Freed Aliens

The Second Galactic Pool Novel

M. Sid Kelly

(Battleship Technician, Second Class, Moth – HANDLE WITH CARE)

ISBN-13: 978-0615993935 (Galactic Pool Publishing)
ISBN-10:0615993931

First Print Edition

DEDICATION

TO MY DAD

CONTENTS

ACKNOWLEDGMENTS

Thanks to my volunteer proofers/editors:
Greg and Julie

You are a Cricket. Do not let the bastards steal that from you.
~ O'Buzznid-3

THE WRONG PLANET

"I have visual confirmation of the target, Captain!"

"Take us in, Pilot," said Captain O'Spotnid-3.

The whole crew stood to study the moonlit geologic formation. They peered into the night through the viewing dome of their uncloaked battleship.

"On screen, Pilot."

Captain O'Spotnid-3 stepped closer to the screen and asked for magnification. "What a bizarre thing this is. When they showed us the training dummy, I thought they were kidding around – just giving the insectoids a little thrill."

"I hope it is not life-sized," said the navigator.

"I believe it is a somewhat inflated representation," said the ship's doctor. "These Dirtlings must have a lot of pride, Captain."

"Yes, Doctor, extraordinary pride... I think we might learn something here, gentlemen. Almost seems a shame… Are we ready?"

"The center of mass is calculated. I make it behind the chin of the tough-looking guy in the back," said the navigator.

"I have verified the center of mass," said the pilot. "We are ready, sir."

"Okay, set weapon on melt."

"Yessir!" replied the pilot.

Captain O'Spotnid-3 paused to consider, one last time, what they were about to do.

Their orders had come directly from the highest levels of the Galactic Pool government. The Vice President himself had hand-selected him.

I should be as proud as these weird people…

But at least he was out of stasis. And he had not chosen mountain melting as a specialty, after all. As far as he was concerned, this was nothing more than an arbitrary situation.

And I just happen to be the one who ended up in it...

That was the most pride-worthy thought he could come up with.

Besides, orders were orders. And he had not been sent to destroy this entire planet – just this tiny bit of it. This maneuver merely symbolized the destruction of every living thing, and the laying to waste of mountain ranges, etcetera. This was nothing more than a diplomatic mission with the simple goal of seeking an amicable compromise. The Dirtlings just needed a foundation upon which a compromise could be built – a nice warm foundation, as the men liked to say. And it was intended to be good for the inhabitants of this backwater in the long run.

"Better than spraying them with poison until they beg for mercy…" he said under his breath.

"Sir?"

"Never mind, Pilot. Fire at will."

The beam hit its spot. The giant faces appeared to blush. And within a few seconds Mount Rushmore had melted into a lava flow.

"Nice work, men! We should have their undivided attention by sunrise. When they arrive, scan their weapon systems, but do not cloak the ship unless-"

Before he could finish his sentence, Captain O'Spotnid-3 saw the glowing landscape turn into a sunlit blue ocean. He felt a slight acceleration as the inertial airbags kicked in. He looked at the view screen and saw ocean swells zipping by beneath his ship.

"REPORT!"

"Sir, we have lost control of the ship!" replied the Click Beetle pilot.

The Dung Beetle navigator pounded on his instrument panel. "Sir, I am unable to verify our position!"

"Engineering! Status!"

"Yes Captain! We have lost power to thrusters, but antimatter is stable. Disconnected… Life support and computer systems normal! Sir, this malfunction appears… almost surgical. Not even a spark…" replied the Bee engineer as he emptied his venom sacs and struggled to keep his stinger in.

The navigator interrupted. "Sir, we are coming in almost parallel to the sea. If we do not contact the surface soon, we may crash into land! One-hundred feet and falling… Ninety-five feet!"

"Pilot! What is our ground speed?"

The Click Beetle pilot called out above the warning siren. "Sir, one-hundred and twenty knots… but… but our outer hull is spinning… at over twenty-five rotations per second, sir!"

"What!?"

"Um, sir," said the navigator. "This is not the same planet. Seventy feet!"

"Not the same planet?"

"Sir, I believe our instruments are functioning properly, but this says we are approximately four-point-three light years from our former location – and now sixty feet above the sea."

"Brace for impact!" called the pilot. "This could get bouncy even with the dampers!"

The Dung Beetle navigator wedged his stubby horn into its holster under the flight console. Captain O'Spotnid-3 poked his leg spikes into their emergency foam stabilization pads. The pilot flipped over on his back and assumed the click position. The Bee engineer grabbed a roll of tape and climbed into the center cell of his honeycomb. The pair of Moth technicians flew around in circles, hoping for the best and shedding beautiful blue and orange scales all over the place.

***

The surfers spotted something as they gazed out to sea looking for the next set of waves. They all pointed their wing tips at a bright object on the horizon. The object did not appear to be moving – at first.

Then one of the surfers said, "Hey, she's getting bigger. She's coming right at us!"

They saw the first splash. Another surfer said, "Can't out-paddle this thing, cats. No need to agitate the gravel..." So they straddled their boards, shook out their feathers, and accepted whatever fate this thing held for them.

The huge disk bounced closer and closer, and got bigger and bigger.

"It looks as though some big honkin' Clyde has flung a gigantramous whacked-out flying saucer at us like a skipping stone," said a third surfer.

Of course, this is exactly what had happened. But no one would believe it for a very long time.

***

"Crew report!" yelled the captain as his ship came to rest, floating about a quarter-mile offshore.

"Sir! The Moth technicians have suffered second degree splats, but I can rebuild them," said the Ant doctor, who had stabilized himself by chomping down onto a bulkhead beam with his heavy duty mandibles.

The Moths were legs-up on the floor with their wings vibrating. The doctor prepared to probaluate them, but first had to stop them spinning in circles.

"Engineering!"

"Sir, the main engine, cloaking device, and weapon systems have been disconnected from the antimatter core somehow. But auxiliary power is one-hundred percent. Life support never even flickered. All other systems appear functional."

"Pilot, send an SOS on all secure channels. Explain our predicament and position in the simplest terms you can."

"Sir, the quantum radio is not functional," said the pilot.

"Engineering, how long for repairs?"

The Bee engineer stood next to a tall transparent cylinder, looking up and down the stacked array of blue antimatter coils inside. He got his buzzing under control and said, "I know the duplicator works, sir. I just repaired my sacs with it. But three antimatter power linkages have been severed. And even though the gap is scarcely a micron wide, I cannot make the duplicator bridge it. It is like the space in between does not actually exist. It seems to be some kind of space-time anomaly or something. Sir, I have no idea…"

"What about the radio?"

"The quantum capacitor appears to exist only in its other place," replied the engineer.

"Navigator, what planet is this?"

"Captain, sir, like the target planet, this planet is not in our database. It is simply too far out. Breathable atmosphere, seventy-seven percent relative gravity… Atmospheric analysis shows a high likelihood of sapient beings with minor amounts of combustion technology."

"Any computer technology?"

"I am scanning… Okay, they have television and radio, but apparently no public computer network. I have TV images confirming combustion/electric technology, sir, but not very advanced and probably not widespread."

"Weapons?"

"Let me flip channels… There is a small hovercraft… I think those things are muffins… Sports… More sports… They apparently like games, sir, and muffins. Little flat boats too... Wait, I think I found the news. This story shows big birds jumping and running around while throwing colorful hoops in the air. Now they are showing something that I can only describe as a patty-cake obstacle course, sir. Now an award ceremony… And this looks like some kind of competitive bake-off. It is all very innocent looking. Wait. Uh, they zoomed in on the muffins and they have something that looks like Ants cooked into the tops. They look just like Doctor Exoskeleton, sir."

"Just how big are these muffins, Navigator?"

The navigator grabbed a frame, enhanced it, and put it up on the view screen.

"They appear to be only slightly larger than standard-sized muffins, and the ants must be tiny – unlikely to be sapient. I do not think these are upright-walking upper-case-A ants, sir," replied the navigator. "The sapient inhabitants, which are large flightless avianoids, would appear to be omnivorous, including insectoids. However, I do not believe we would be at risk of predation from them if we left the ship."

"I do not plan to leave the ship, Navigator. I plan to be on our way back to the target planet to complete our mission shortly," said Captain O'Spotnid-3. "Engineering! Update our status!"

The two Moth technicians were back to normal and one of them had joined the Bee engineer crawling around in the pit below the antimatter chamber.

"We are giving it all we got, sir! We have tried to link the plasma field connections, but there is nothing to attach to. It is like a two-dimensional wormhole. That micron gap might be light years wide in reality, sir. I am going to need a lot of conduit."

"How about the radio?"

"We have recovered the quantum capacitor's information, but we are not optimistic about reassembling it. One of the Moths is making an attempt."

The Moth technician tapped away at a keyboard as a series of different-colored block-like shapes cascaded down the screen. He attempted to arrange them at the bottom as they fell, but he was leaving a lot of gaps.

"Alright, the threat from outside… Report!"

The Dung Beetle navigator replied. "Sir, their television broadcasts show no sign of weaponry or aircraft. I do not think we need to worry about being swooped down upon by a military or anything."

The Click Beetle pilot interrupted. "Sir! Look outside."

The entire crew looked out to see a group of very large shaggy birds on little flat boats. They were using their wings to paddle toward the floating super saucer.

"Uh oh, here come the locals. Are the grabber beams online?"

"Yessir!" replied the pilot.

"Hit them with an egocite stream, but do not let them get any closer than ear shot."

The pilot turned on the outside audio receiver and then used a grabber beam to form an invisible egocite delivery tube. As the egocite vapor saturated the verbal regions of the avianoids' brains, the galactic autotranslator kicked in and the crew listened.

"HONK HONK HONK… wonder what those space bugs eat?" asked one of the avianoid surfers as he pointed up at the insectoid crew peering down from the ship's viewing dome.

"Yipes! That one red hoedad has got some chomps!"

"This is the biggest hovercraft ever!" said another surfer. "Cats, this ride is bigger than my whole barrio!"

"Not much of a hovercraft, if you ask me, daddy-o. More of a skippercraft, I'd call it," replied the largest surfer – the one they call Dayv.

The other surfers laughed.

But another creature had been attracted by the flying saucer's crash landing.

The insectoid crew saw it rise from the depths. It was just a giant head at first – the body was still too deep to see.

The water erupted under the surfers and feathers exploded into the air.

"SQUAAAAAAAAAAUK!" yelled a stricken surfer as a full-grown adult short-necked plesiosaur dove back under the waves with a severed leg and half a surfboard in its mouth.

"Encase them!" said Captain O'Spotnid-3.

The pilot wrapped them in a grabber beam just in time for the plesiosaur to attack again. The monster appeared to clamp its mouth around the entire mid-section of the biggest surfer, but it came away empty."

"Hold them until the beast loses interest, Pilot."

"Captain, with all due respect, that person is bleeding to death!" said the doctor.

They watched as the surfers applied pressure to the victim's femoral artery in an effort to slow the blood loss. One of the surfers was attempting to use the leash of his board as a tourniquet, but there was no stump to attach too.

"I see that, Doctor. But these are sentient beings on an uncontacted planet. I cannot bring them aboard for a mere bleeding-to-death."

They paused to watch the plesiosaur return. It attempted to batter the surfers with its tail. The surfers honked bloody murder. But the animal could not touch them.

"We caused this, Captain. We – that is, I am obligated to care for the victim."

The plesiosaur attempted to bite each surfer in succession. Each surfer freaked out appropriately. The victim appeared to be unconscious.

"Doctor Exoskeleton, I believe that we will ultimately do more harm than good if we abduct that fellow. That is why it is against the law for us to interact with them."

They saw the plesiosaur's head burst from the red water as if looking for its best shot. It turned, dove, and attempted to grab the victim from below again. But it smacked its head on the grabber beam envelope and sank to the bottom.

"We have ALREADY interacted with them, Captain. Pilot, bring them aboard and place them in sickbay," ordered Doctor Exoskeleton.

The Click Beetle pilot looked at his captain.

Captain O'Spotnid-3 said, "Doctor Exoskeleton makes a good point. Do as he says, Pilot."

"Yessir!" said the pilot as he grabber-beamed the surfers up in one big wet bloody pile.

"Whoa, daddy-o," said one surfer as the flock tried to arrange itself on the slippery floor of the ship's sickbay.

Doctor Exoskeleton dosed them with calming agent. Then he isolated the plesiosaur attack victim and clamped the leg wound shut with his mandibles while the Moths fired up the medical duplicator. He stabilized the victim, sealed the wound, and provided him with duplicated blood. The Moths had the mess cleaned up even before the captain came in.

"Welcome aboard. I am Captain O'Spotnid-3, but you can call me Captain Spotty, or just Captain, if you have trouble with insectoid names. We are tending to your stricken comrade – he should be fine momentarily. But I apologize for not knowing how to greet you properly, for we seem to have landed not where we would have intended. The inhabitants of our original target planet would have expected 'Take me to your leader' as a greeting."

The surfers all looked at Dayv.

"I guess that'd be yours-truly in a pinch. I look to be the senior cat of this cool band of brothers, Mon Capitan. But is my fine-feathered-shredder going to be a complete cock again, daddy-o?"

Captain Spotty replied, looking bewildered. "Um, I am not sure what, um… Do you speak an allegorical language of some kind? Our autotranslator is still getting warmed up, perhaps?"

"Oh, sorry Cap'n," said Dayv. "Cats, our new friends don't speak hipster. You need to speak like they are your mothers."

All ten guys nodded at Dayv.

"So Cap'n, I am Dayv. We don't have an overall country-wide leader-type-person that we could take you to. But we'd be happy to introduce you to our wives. You will be welcomed as honored and very curious guests. Though we do wonder what it is you chow upon… I mean, what do you eat?"

"We were wondering the same about you. We have seen your muffin toppings…" said Captain Spotty.

The group of surfers, including the plesiosaur attack victim, laughed.

"Gotcha Cap'n. There's no threat from us. Nobody's going to scarf you here. There are the sea beasts, as you saw, but our ancestors skee-daddled most of the big land predators a few generations back. You cats do look like big ol' muffin decorations though. You just have to make sure a big ol' bronto doesn't step on you, or worse, in the forest. They're pretty easy to spot though."

"That is comforting, Mister Dayv. You are also safe around us. We eat a variety of foodstuffs, but we get all of our food from our ship's duplicators. Well, except for him," said Captain Spotty, indicating the navigator.

The navigator lowered his horn and raised a claw in sheepish admission.

Captain Spotty continued. "So, speaking of duplicators, the doctor needs to replace your comrade's missing leg. Doctor?"

"Yes, Mister Victim, you have some options for your repairs. We can duplicate your left leg and attach it to your right hip. It will be functional, but you will have two left legs. It might take some getting used to. And you may never dance again."

The surfers stood with their beaks agape, staring in disbelief at the doctor.

"Or we can duplicate one of your friends' right legs and just fit it to your right socket. In which case, you should try to choose a donor to match your own dimensions as closely as possible." The doctor scanned the options and pointed at one of the other surfers. "I would recommend him."

The victim propped himself up on his side, supported his head with his wing, and examined the candidate. The candidate spun in a circle and did a couple of deep knee bends.

"Or, if you desire, we can give you a full pair of one of your friends' legs. In this case, you can select anyone you like. Perhaps you would like to be even taller."

"Dayv...?" said the victim.

"Me? Yo, daddy-o, I'm not exactly a squab anymore…"

"I know, Dayv, but it would be an honor, big cat, really and righteously… Plus, you shred like a penguin, and the hens dig your drumsticks. I could do some super jumps with your pegs on my bod."

With an efficiency that precluded letting the conversation continue, the doctor shined a laser pointer at Dayv and said, "Replace both of the victim's legs with duplicates of this donor's legs from his pygostyle down. This will not hurt either of you."

There was an audible 'plop'. A Moth technician had grabber-beamed off the plesiosaur victim's remaining leg. The leg appeared to jump into the matter conversion hopper of its own volition. And a moment later, duplicates of Dayv's legs appeared in the medical duplicator bin. The Moth technician used a grabber beam to unwrap the stumps and attach them to the victim with two more plops. They waved an auto-suture wand over the seams and told the victim to wiggle his talons.

The doctor said, "I used your own leg matter in the new leg duplication, which should decrease the weirdness factor by approximately thirty percent for you."

"Try 'em out, Blood Brother!" said Dayv.

The victim stood with apparent ease. He jumped and bonked his head on the viewing dome. "Fab! Thanks Dayv! These are awesome!" He strutted around the sickbay like the rooster that he was – his new legs making up three-quarters of his new total body mass. He almost tripped over one of the Moth technicians.

"So, Mister Dayv, how long until someone official gets here to investigate us, and what should we expect?" asked Captain Spotty. "Things get tricky for us once we have had traceable contact with beings of an otherwise uncontacted world. You may, by default, end up a member of our Galactic Pool."

"Cap'n, we are already investigating you, so I'm not sure if I understand the question. Are YOU speaking in allegories now? And besides, this Galactic Pool thing you have here looks wicked! What's the trick?"

"Mister Dayv, are you saying nobody could have seen us besides you fellows? There is no radar or other detection system?"

"That's pretty much probably right, Cap'n."

The other surfers confirmed this fact with shrugs and confused looks.

"You just came down from outer space right out there, right? You haven't been elsewhere?" asked Dayv.

"Honestly? A few moments ago we were over four light years' worth of elsewhere."

"I take it that means 'no'. And yes, it's pretty remote out here. Listen – can't even hear the hens honking… That's why we're here – just me and the boys hanging out at my cabin and shredding at our favorite break. Sometimes I bring some squabs from the orphanage down here to look at the tidepools and camp out and stuff, but otherwise it's just us. So come on over! We'll have a beach bonfire. What kinds of instruments do you cats play?"

"Uh, I rub my wings together a little, and my Click Beetle pilot is an accomplished percussionist... We appreciate the invitation, however we need to make repairs and be on our way. Central Command did not issue us a memory wiper unit for this mission. We usually just melt things – and there is no need to cover your tracks when you get to that point. So we are going to have to ask you not to say anything about this encounter."

"But how am I going to explain Dayv's legs on my body?" asked the plesiosaur victim.

"Blood, the hens never noticed your sticks before, right? So how they gonna know the difference? Just tell them you've been working out. Besides, Cap'n, nobody'd believe this crazy story anyway."

"We appreciate your discretion and your hospitality. I will offer to get you back to shore using our grabber beam with the sea beast still around. So if you will excuse us, we have much work to do," said Captain Spotty.

"Cap'n, this has been a real treat for us cats. We've learned a lot – secrets of the universe kind of stuff."

The 'cats' all nodded their enthusiastic agreement.

"So, here, allow me to present you with this."

Dayv removed his plesiosaur tooth necklace and placed it around Captain Spotty's cephalothorax.

"A reminder of Mother Roost!" Dayv said. "We'll look for you in the morning, but I expect to see nothing out here but tasty waves – so I'll say bon voyage Cap'n. However, if you castaways are still casted away, then you have to promise to call upon us at my humble abode."

Captain Spotty, ever the diplomat and confident that his crew would make the repairs, made the promise.

***

That evening, while the crew busted their malpighian tubules trying to fix the ship, Captain and Doctor had a captain/doctor conversation in the canteen.

"Exoskeleton, I WILL get my men home, and I DO intend to complete my mission."

"I am sure the men would agree, Spotty. But you do have to consider how to handle things if we are marooned for some period of time. This ship is going to start feeling pretty small."

"Our world is on this ship. This ship IS the Galactic Pool as far as I am concerned. I may have to visit our hosts on shore as protocol dictates, but the crew will remain on board at all times. Just because we happen to be floating in their ocean, it does not mean that we are in their world – it does not mean we can start going around having campfire jamdowns on alien worlds. The men are not permitted to visit other planets outside of the Galactic Pool at any other time, so they just have to imagine themselves to be light years away from this place."

"You have a good crew, Spotty – the best in the fleet. They will accept this for a long time, I expect. But at some point, if we are still here…"

"Then, Exoskeleton, we will sink this ship and become food for the fishes."

Besmirch not cannibalism. For how many Crickets can one galaxy hold?
~ O'Buzznid-3

CRICKETS AND BEARS

"How many kittens this time, Daddy?!" asked Dee's youngest cub, who was lying on his back on the mat inside the family wrestling room.

"How many do you want?"

"Eleventy-thousand!"

"Cubby, that's a lot of kittens. How many did you wrestle last time?"

"Eleventy-hundred, Daddy!"

"HAHAHA! Yay, Cubby, that's a lot! Did you win?"

"Yes Daddy! Remember? I won right away – they pinned me in like a second. I bet eleventy-thousand would flatten me. It would be sooo fun!"

"Okay, how about if I send in eleventy-dozen? Is that enough?"

"I think so, Daddy! That sure is a lot!"

Dee pulled a cord and over a hundred kittens slid down a chute right onto the cub. Kittens spilled all around the little Bear. Some of the kittens seemed to figure out that it was a wrestling match right away. They swatted at the cub's ears and toes, and also at each other. Some of the kittens tried to wander off. Dee scooped the strays up and added them back to the pile on top of his cub.

"Okay son, be careful with your rolling around. Let the kittens come to you!"

"YAY! They are so fuzzy! I think they have me pinned. Do they have me pinned, Daddy?"

"Almost! Okay – how does it feel now?"

"Warm and fuzzy and very tickly, Daddy!"

"I think you won! I can't see you at all. They totally have you pinned! Okay, Son, count to a hundred now," said Dee.

The little cub counted to a hundred – not including the thirties – and then jumped up in a victory pose. Several kittens still clung to his fur, and one sat atop his head.

Dee and his cub gathered up the kittens. Dee said, "I bet that made you hungry, huh?"

"Yes, Daddy, and I bet it made the kittens hungry too."

"You are right, I think. How about if you go on and find your sister? I bet Mommy has something nice for you to eat. And I'll feed the kittens."

"Yes, Daddy!"

His cub galloped toward the ranch house, and Dee went to the feed warehouse.

***

Dee heard the phone in his office ring. Shirtless and wearing blue jeans, he dropped a one-hundred-pound sack from his massive shoulder into a feed hopper, brushed the dust from his chest fur, and then sat down at his desk.

"Hugs to you. This is Dee."

"Yes, Mister Dee-Ay-En-15? Proprietor of Kitten Emporium?"

"Yep, that's me. What can I do for you, buddy?" Dee activated the video panel.

"I have a special delivery, sir."

"Hey! A Cockroach! You look just like my old cousin Buzzy! Gosh I miss him. He was the best Cockroach ever…"

"Sir, I am a Cricket, as was General O'Buzznid-3."

"Oh," replied Dee. "Wait, did you say 'General'? Uh, Buzzy was just a PLUMBOB computer text translator, so, sorry, you have the wrong address."

"General O'Buzznid-3 wore many hats, sir. In fact, this is a delivery FROM your cousin," said the cargo ship captain.

"Gosh, I'm not expecting anything from him. Because… well… poor Buzzy is… dead." Dee tried to disguise his sobbing as coughing, but the galactic autotranslator betrayed him.

"Yes, of course he is, sir. Else my delivery would be unnecessary. Allow me to show you the note."

The Cricket captain pulled up an electronic document and displayed it on Dee's video panel. Written in Bearish, the note read:

I, O'Buzznid-3, being of sound mind and itchy head, do record my last will and testament. My only personal possession, my stasis case, I leave to Trukk-9 because he already has it. My private files on Planet One may have some value to historians; however, they do not belong to me to bequeath. As for family concerns, I have but one living relative. So, in the event that their mother is unable to find them adequate rearing habitat before she completes her life cycle, I bequeath the care of my grubs to my cousin, Mister Dee-Ay-En-15.

"What!? I'm not his cousin. Look at me. I'm a Bearman for crying out loud. This is obviously a mistake, right?" Dee stood up in front of the video console to model his obvious Bearman features.

"No, sir. You are legally registered as his cousin and only known living relative. And you are legally required to accept this delivery. If you do not accept delivery immediately, you are obliged to pay my port fees as I wait. I also have a six-pack of Tiger Beetle enforcement agents that I am required to thaw out if you refuse delivery."

"What kind of stupid law is that!? Besides, you don't understand. I was only his JOKING cousin." Dee tried to explain the custom that he and Buzzy had encountered on a planet called Earth, and that they'd had tremendous fun playing the joking cousin game.

"It is not a law that I can overrule. Are you able to take delivery now?"

"Delivery of child Crickets?! Now? How many are we talking?"

The cargo ship captain shuffled through some receipts. "Let us see… doot doot… Two teenagers…"

"Two teenagers!? That's insane! I don't know anything about raising teenagers."

"Sir, no one does. Please allow me to finish. I have a consignment of two teens and… doot doot… one-hundred and twelve grubs."

"Wait a second! WAIIIIT just a second, buddy. TEENagers are too old. They couldn't be Buzzy's children. See? You've brought them to the wrong guy."

"We Crickets develop quickly if not contained in stasis. They are teens in Cricket years. They should not be a problem, sir. They will occasionally make sudden and erratic movements, and they can eat a lot, but they do not require much care other than perhaps a good hosing down once in a while. And you can always put them back into their stasis boxes when they need a time-out."

"But the babies – a hundred babies…?"

"Sir, all you have to do is let them loose on the land. If any survive, they will come back as teens after they complete their final instar stage."

"I can't let baby Crickets roam free here. The kittens will hunt them. Kittens might be cute, but they are merciless."

"That is to be expected, sir. Few Crickets must survive to adulthood. We need predators to control our numbers. This is the natural way."

"They'll be slaughtered!"

"Think about it, sir. If every baby Cricket survived, the galaxy would soon be filled with Crickets."

"Oh. But what about their mother?"

"Their mother completed her life cycle, of course. The grubs could not be allowed to infest the space station where they were born. She was only authorized to release two grubs into the space station's biopods. Those two became these teens. And she put the rest of the grubs into stasis… for you, sir."

"What about HER relatives?"

"Unknown, sir. She was just a radio voice on a distant space station."

"Oh. What do they eat then?"

"Pretty much anything. If you choose to feed them, they will eat whatever you feed the kittens. If you choose not to feed them, they will scrounge on the land and/or eat each other."

"Okay, okay, but are you sure I have to take delivery? I don't think it's in the best interest of the children. Can't you declare me incompetent or something?"

"Sir, our records show that you raise and sell thousands of kittens. Crickets will be a piece of cake. Please authorize me to land on your property and we can begin the transfer."

***

The cargo ship touched down on the back-forty of Dee's ranch. An Ant stevedore unloaded a pallet of small Cricket cases, each about the size of a shoebox. Then he rolled the two full-sized teenager cases down the ramp with a grabber beam dolly. The ship's captain came out to greet Dee.

"Sir, may I recommend that we simply open the cases here and let the grubs go free on the land? I am authorized to provide you with this assistance. Reviving static insectoids can be hazardous if done incorrectly."

"OHHH yeah, buddy – I know a little bit about that. But I can't let the poor things fend for themselves out here. You're right – I have the facilities to rear them up until they are ready to go home."

"Home, sir?"

"Yeah, back to ZZZZZZ-3 where they belong."

"I am afraid that they are citizens of Free-15, sir. If they want to apply for visas when they reach two years, they may be permitted to visit ZZZZZZ-3 like anyone else. But ZZZZZZ-3 is not a place where they would want to live. It remains a war poisoned wasteland. The vast majority of insectoids now live elsewhere in the Galactic Pool."

"But once they are full grown, there's no way I can adequately house them all," said Dee.

"Precisely," said the cargo ship captain.

"How long can they stay in these little boxes?"

"Indefinitely. General O'Buzznid-3 himself spent periods spanning decades in his box. He is your cousin, sir – you do not know anything about who he was?"

"No, not really... He was just a little guy who was fun to play with. He was pretty good at translating text and all that, but he could be a little surly at times."

"Unfortunately, I am not authorized to teach you insectoid history. Anyway, I would unpack the teenagers first. They will be of assistance once you decide to release the grubs. Okay, if I can get you to sign here, sir…"

Dee signed the documents and said, "My wife isn't going to be happy about this, but I think the cubs will enjoy the challenges of Cricket wrestling. Buzzy was a pretty fair wrestler, but he was what I would call a reluctant warrior."

"That he was, sir. That he was… By the way – and I am not actually allowed to say this, so please do not tell anyone – you should get a copy of General O'Buzznid-3's memoir. It is called 'I, Buzzy'. It has, of course, been banned by the Planet One administration, but I know a secure site where you can download a copy of the ebook for only ninety-nine cents. I will send you a link. Please read it to the children so they at least know of their honorable father."

***

Dee was very careful when he released the teenagers. It took the young Crickets a few minutes to warm up and regain all of their senses. They bounced around some, but they didn't cause any damage. They finally greeted Dee with the customary Cricket bows.

"Welcome to Free-15, little nephews!" said Dee as he hugged them together. "Do you fellows have any idea what's going on here?"

"I am not a fellow. I am a girl. He is a boy. Yes, we know who you are, Uncle. Will you be releasing our brothers and sisters soon?"

"Whoa, whoa... Yeah, but let's talk about it first. Are you young Crickets ready to be raised by Bears? I mean, I'm sure it's a whole lot different than what you are supposed to live like. We are pretty rough-and-tumble, and we say a lot of things that you'd never hear insectoids say."

"Our father insisted that we would be happier as Bears. Mother said that his last words were 'Make them be Bears'. Apparently, he knew you would keep and raise all of us. He seemed to think this was important," said the girl Cricket.

The young male reached out a claw and said, "My name is O'Buzznid-3 Junior, and my sister is Miss O'Buzzelda. But you can call us Buzzy and Buzzel if you have trouble with insectoid names."

"Oh, no. No, no. I can't call you Buzzy. There's already too much confusion in the Galactic Pool with all the crazy names. Do you know that I have a friend named Dluhosh-10!? I mean, when I say that name – when I can remember it – it almost gives me a hemorr-"

"Yes, we understand," interrupted Miss O'Buzzelda. "Please, it is within your rights to name us whatever you choose. In fact, you will need to come up with names for all of the grubs if you plan to raise them."

"How about if I just call you Zelda and Buster? Those are good solid Bear names. And my name is Dee. Um, we should probably get some kitten chow ready for you and the brood, huh?"

"Yes, Uncle Dee, I can smell the food and it is making me hungry," said Buster.

"Uncle? You knew our father?" asked Zelda.

"Oh yes, I knew him well. Well, I thought I knew him well. But that nice cargo ship captain didn't seem to think so. He said that your pop wrote a book and that I should read it to you. Would you like to hear it while you eat?"

"Yes please," they both replied.

Dee downloaded the file and opened it in his ereader. He began reading aloud.

Foreword.
I, Buzzy, am a fu-

"Whoa! HAAHAA! Oh boy, your daddy sure was fond of saying that! I guess he was right though. All along I thought he was just a delusional Cockroach. Um, anyway, I'll keep it clean for you, okay?" He began reading again.

I, Buzzy, am a 'freaking' *Cricket.*
Yes, I know that this is a rudely harsh and shocking way to begin a memoir – especially for a decorated career bureaucrat Cricket like myself. But I have reasons to shock you into attention – reasons which I hope will be clear in the words I write herein. I shall not use such vile language again, but I want this memoir to be charged with an undercurrent of shock.

"HA! I like that 'charged with an undercurrent of shock' bit. See what he did there?" said Dee. "Such a clever Cricket… Okay…"

Chapter 1.
I was born on ZZZZZZ-3 before the war.
How is that possible, you may ask.
Stasis. A lot of stasis.
As a teen, I enlisted to fight in the Insectoidicide War against Planet One – the so-called ZZZZZZ-3 Liberation Action. By the end of the war, I was a general officer in command of the elite Tiger Beetle Brigade. And, yes, I was present at the signing of the Treaty of Do What We Say. This was to be the greatest humiliation of my many humiliations. I hope for, but do not expect, your forgiveness for agreeing to sign this evil document. You can see illustrations of me in

the Great Library's historic drawing collection adding my signature. Subsequently, our people were spared further chemical warfare. But to what end? This?

Dee paused again. "Boy, I sure hope all of his chapters are that short. I hate big blocks of italicized text – takes me right out of the story. Plus it won't let me change the font. Anyway…"

Chapter 2.

I write this memoir on my free time during what I expect will be my final mission.

"Hey! That's the mission he was on with me. I wondered why he always made excuses when I invited him to wrestle. He sure seemed glad when the mission ended even though he… Oh, you guys probably don't want to know about that stuff yet…" Dee continued reading.

I have begun shedding my leg spikes and the head itch has intensified rapidly. I only derive a small quantity of satisfaction from scratching it myself. I need a woman, and soon. Any hungry woman will do at this point. I must soon complete my life cycle, or, alternatively, I will lose my sanity and become unfit for further service as I suffer a lingering death.

In actual fact, I have written this memoir in my mind. You see, I was placed into stasis so many times that I eventually learned to retain mental consciousness while my physical body shut down. Between assignments for various vice presidents, I have spent most of the past several decades in my box thinking. Now it is a simple matter to dictate these words to myself.

I was placed into stasis for the first time right after the Treaty was signed. Planet One placed every insectoid who held an office or a leadership position into stasis immediately after our surrender. They were not yet sure of how best to use us, and they did not want us to influence the general insectoid population while they were being re-purposed to serve Planet One.

I was eventually appointed Personal Cricket to the Vice President, and was used for any task he deemed top priority. For example, I was the Cricket who released the ceremonial mouse at every presidential inauguration since the inception of the Galactic Pool. I think they used me because they liked my general's hat. In fact, at Rim Ram-1's inauguration, he said to me, "I like your hat." At Gren Wee-1's inauguration, he said to me, "Heh-heh, a Cricket in a hat is like a Swamp Master in a wetsuit." I still do not know what he meant, but I stopped wearing my hat after that.

After each task – usually something brief and ceremonial or diplomatic, and often only lasting a few hours – I was placed back into stasis. Some vice presidents found little or no use for me, however. During one stretch, I administered the mouse at three consecutive inaugurations without ever doing a vice presidential task in between.

Some of the longer and more notable missions that I will detail later in this memoir include these: I commanded the Ant Police in the arrest of the Fermamentian King after the egocite mine scandal, as seen in Trukk-9's masterpiece. I worked as a PLUMBOB agent during the evaluation of Dnooblia-10. And I oversaw the top secret installation of the second-generation galactic autotranslator.

"Hey," said Dee. "That means your daddy knew where that damned galactic autotranslator was the whole time I knew him! Why didn't he tell me? He knew that I REALLY want to take a dump on that sucker! Oh well, I can keep dreaming. Anyway…"

Chapter 3.
Vice President Griffplbbbbb…

"Griffblbbbbb? What?"

Dee scrolled down. "Gosh darn it children, it looks like the formatting's all messed up. All the way down… It's just… Oh, here can you read this?"

Dee moved his head so that Buster and Zelda could see the ereader screen.

"No, Uncle. This is not Cricketish. I do not know what it is," replied Zelda through a mouth full of kitten food.

"You know what? I bet you five bucks it's that damn galactic autotranslator that messed this up. And too bad – it looked like Buzzy was going to say something about Vice President Griffer-1. I know that guy. He's a di-"

Just then Dee's two cubs came galloping into the office. "Daddy! Daddy! Mommy got us some honey!"

"Oh boy, my cubbies! I just love honey!"

Dees cubs noticed the Crickets and jumped behind their daddy's massive legs.

"HAAHAA! Oh, little cubbies… It's okay! These two fine Crickets are your cousins! Go ahead and give them hugs. Just watch out for their leg spikes."

I am almost three feet tall, armor plated, heavily spiked, and I can bite through sheet metal. I can kick the ass of any humanoid I have ever met. But still they smirk.

~ O'Buzznid-3

OLD FRIENDS, AS IT WERE

Dluhosh-X relaxed after another productive day on Earth. He was worn out from trying to cure malaria, spraying calming agent on some warring factions, vanquishing a few more human traffickers, and taking his weekly blacksmithing lessons. He stowed his tongs and his new sledgehammer, which he could wield with one tentacle even though it had a twenty-pound head and a handle almost as tall as he was.

He gave all ten of is tentacles and their interconnecting hood a good stretching out, then he let his normally traffic-cone shaped body melt into a blob in his pilot's chair. He tuned into American TV, which he had been enjoying more and more as the galactic autotranslator got the bizarre language dialed in. The image on the screen was the view from a helicopter of a featureless gray landscape with spots of smoke rising from here and there. It reminded Dluhosh of one of the four Great Melted Mountain National Parks of the Galactic Pool.

"Oops," he said.

The news anchor – the lumpy one named Marie with the blonde hair and boney knees that Dluhosh could hardly stand to look at – comes on and says, "Again, if you are just joining us, Mount Rushmore has melted. Yes, I said melted. Take a look at these live images."

The view reverts to the aerial footage of the devastation. Then it cuts back to Marie with a full body shot as she walks over to the studio roundtable, skirt well above the knee and lumps highlighted.

Dluhosh gagged just a little. He tasted sour anchovy in the back of his throat.

Marie continues. "Authorities are investigating, but experts have not reached a conclusion about how this happened. We have assembled a panel of our own experts to discuss various possible causes, and since we are interrupting taping of Daytime Today Daily, we may take some questions from the studio audience. So, to my far left we have Mister Bob Gnobbler, founder of the Institute for Non-Coincidence Studies. Good to see you again, Bob."

"Thanks Marie. It's always a pleasure."

"And next to Bob we have Doctor Oscar Boston, a physicalist with advanced degrees from several big schools. Welcome Doctor."

Doctor Boston, wearing a brown corduroy sport coat, said, "Thank you, Marie. That's 'physicist' by the way."

"Sure. And to my right you'll recognize the host of the hit show *Grab That Thing Before It Gets Away!* – Merle 'Doc' Maudlin! How's it goin', Doc?"

"Great, Marie! Glad to be here! Looks like the so-called authorities failed to grab that thing before it got away!" he says as he strikes his trademark strangle-hold pose with flexed biceps bulging out from below his torn-off sleeves. The studio audience hoots its approval and many of them imitate the pose.

Marie continues. "And next to him we have the Reverend Grace Goonch of the Church of Holy Wholeness. Thanks for being here Grace."

"Thanks for having me here on this wholly holy occasion." Grace is wearing an ankle-length skirt and neck-high blouse, which is much easier on Dluhosh's stomach.

"Okay, let's begin with you, Doctor Boston. What does science say happened here?"

"I'm not aware that any actual science has been done yet, Marie. But we may be able to formulate some hypotheses. For example, the Yellowstone Caldera lies to the west of Mount Rushmore…"

Marie shrugs at the audience to comfort the ones who are already lost.

"… and that region is highly volcanic. We do not precisely know the extent of volcanic influence of the caldera on the overlying bedrock. I think it would be reasonable to begin with a hypothesis of some volcanic cause for this phenomenon. But there's still a lot we don't know, so anything I say is just speculation at this point..."

'Doc' Maudlin interrupts. "What we have here, Marie, is final proof of something our government has known for a long time. Space aliens are here on Earth. Whatever alien force this was, it came from above, which, as we all know, is exactly where space aliens come from. We need to mobilize and…" 'Doc' Maudlin pauses to point at the studio audience.

"GRAB THAT THING BEFORE IT GETS AWAY!" they yell.

Doctor Boston says, "That explanation requires a very complex scenario, including an advanced alien race travelling light years across space just to melt Mount Rushmore. Have you not heard of Occam's Razor? I think we are safer in starting with a simpler hypothesis – something to do with the quite common phenomenon of volcanism, for example." Doctor Boston is obviously agitated.

'Doc' Maudlin smiles and winks as he pantomimes strangling Doctor Boston. The audience eats it up.

The Reverend Goonch says, "I see the Hand of The Almighty in this work. That mountain was a monument to liberalism, as we all know. So He chose to smite it. I see this as a stern admonition that we leave behind the evil stench of creeping socialism."

Doctor Boston sighs and says, "Are you sure The Almighty didn't think the mountain was a monument to gay polygamy?"

The Reverend Goonch raises her eyebrows and pooches out her lips as if she's considering it.

Bob Gnobbler chimes in. "There you go with the Hand of The Almighty again, Grace. What you fail to understand is that this was an inside job – that much is the truth. What we've witnessed here is something that my people have been warning of for years. The ionosphere has already been turned against the workers, and now we've witnessed the next phase. It wasn't a matter of IF, but WHEN. And my people documented extraordinary aerial spraying activity in that region recently. You want the answer? Look no farther than the puppet masters in the Pentagon who control, and have always controlled, our illegitimate government."

Doctor Boston plants his palm on his forehead, rolls his eyes, and says, "Jeez, next you'll have someone in here saying it was melted by a bigfoot."

"Bigfoot!?" says 'Doc' Maudlin. "You are out of your mind, Professor! Bigfoot? Son, Bigfoot is a primitive ape-man. There ain't no WAY and no HOW that Bigfoot could have anything at all to do with the melting of Mount Rushmore. Leave him outta this. Some of his relatives may have perished in this tragedy. Have you no respect? You eggheads are psychos!"

Doctor Boston walks off the set in a huff. An audience member yells, "Grab that thing before it gets away!" to the obvious delight of 'Doc' Maudlin.

Dluhosh flipped channels and turned on his scanner to see whether Planet One's mountain melter ship was broadcasting its message of compromise yet. Historically, they would have begun diplomacy as soon as the public was aware of the melted mountain. He wondered what was delaying them. Then it occurred to him that Pixel Person ULBTX-123 might be involved.

***

Dluhosh piloted his ship to Michael's house. There were two cars in the driveway, neither of which looked familiar. But both guys were in the house glued to the television watching images of Reverend Grace Goonch and Bob Gnobbler, who appeared ready to throw chairs at each other. Gregory had a wiener dog on his lap. Both guys wore baggy sweat pants, hoodies and untied basketball shoes. Michael wore a blue baseball cap high on his head and skewed to the side.

Dluhosh could see them through the front window, so he broke it out with a grabber beam and abducted all three of them and their couch onto his cloaked ship.

The look of terror on their faces disappeared as soon as Dluhosh reinstated their memories of the previous abduction, and, of course, applied calming agent. The dog, named Miles, stopped barking at Dluhosh.

Michael said, "We need calming agent!"

"You've already had a triple dose," said Dluhosh.

Gregory said, "We Earthlings have a very high tolerance, remember?"

So Dluhosh dosed them again. Both guys sat there shaking their heads and laughing. Miles rolled over and wiggled around on his back.

"Well, Mister Ammonite, those Planet One assholes really did it, didn't they?" said Michael.

"It would appear so," said Dluhosh.

"Hey, what are you still doing here anyway?" asked Gregory.

"Wait a second," said Michael. "Are you the one who's been wiping out malaria? And what about all those dismembered and disemboweled human traffickers? Was that you too? A lot of people have been blaming space aliens for a lot of things lately."

"Yes… You could say that I've been enjoying the life of a rogue Dnooblian who is making a difference in the world. All of those sudden cease-fires too – the warring factions just needed a little calming agent. Anyway, ULBTX-123 got upset and stranded me here after we dropped you off. So I decided to stick around. Now I'm afraid he'll twist this latest invasion into being YOUR fault somehow. He'll want to blame someone, so let's get you out of here before he hurls an asteroid at your house."

"You mean 'out of here' as in leave Earth again?" asked Michael.

"Yes, I think it's time that I head back to Dnooblia. You want to go?"

"Only if I can bring my dog," said Gregory.

"Wait a sec. Let's think about this," said Michael. "Dluhosh, bro, do you see those cars?"

"Bro?"

"Yeah, 'bro'."

"You never used to say that," said Dluhosh.

"Right, but, you know, we cashed in those golden flip-flops and got these cars. Check 'em out," said Gregory.

"Simply put, bro, we are cooler now. We have special ladies too. Well, almost. Gregory almost has one," said Michael.

"Are you sure you guys are cool?" asked Dluhosh, displaying a faint orange tint of awkwardness.

"Sure. I'm cool, right Gregory?"

"You are coolER."

"You too, bro."

"See? So yeah, we are kind of cool now, you know. We still like bugs and stuff, but we learned to keep them separate from potential special ladies," said Gregory.

"Is this just an Earthling thing? Because to me, it seems like YOUR 'special ladies' should also be into bugs and stuff. And please stop using the word 'bro' or else I'm not taking you anywhere."

"Well, Gregory, what would cool guys do?" asked Michael.

"Cool guys would definitely go to Dnooblia. The special ladies just have to understand."

"Okay, we're in," said Michael.

"Fine. Let's just get a safe distance from Earth, and figure out what to do next."

***

Dluhosh piloted his ship to the safe side of the moon and said, "Okay, ULBTX-123 knows it was Planet One that melted the mountain. The battleship did not initiate diplomacy, so I think ULBTX-123 must have detected and disposed of it. Earth is probably safe from Planet One now.

However, Planet One is likely in grave danger from our big-voiced friend."

"Screw 'em," said Michael.

"It's not that simple. If he decides to hit Planet One with an asteroid, it would kill many innocent people from all over the Galactic Pool. So what I propose is that I try to get his attention. If he isn't already destroying Planet One, he may be monitoring this sector closely for additional invaders."

"I thought you said he would blame us?" said Michael.

"If we get his attention purposefully, and explain the situation – maybe apologize for not stopping the battleship – he won't have to come looking for you. I think revealing ourselves on our terms would make you safer, actually."

"That sounds pretty risky, Dluhosh," said Gregory. "That guy is goofy. I don't trust him. No way."

"But we really need to stop him doing anything rash against Planet One. Here..." Dluhosh gave them a presumably sub-lethal dose of calming agent, Miles excluded.

"Yeah, sure," said Gregory, sinking deeper into the couch.

"Yeah," said Michael before he gave an involuntary snort. "But you know it's just going to turn into an argument with him."

"That's probably going to be your fault though. You two love picking at some point and just being contrary for the sake of being contrary."

"No we don't," said Gregory.

"See? You can't even help it. If we contact him and it isn't too late, we might be able to manipulate him into cooperating. Just use flattery rather than argument, okay? Plus, he can get us to Dnooblia instantly."

"And what if that big-voice asshole decides to smash us?" asked Michael.

Dluhosh turned up the calming agent dial another couple of notches.

Gregory, barely able to wipe his nose on this sleeve, said, "It is a good day to die."

Dluhosh switched off his cloaking device and expelled rhythmic bursts of antimatter tachyon plasma.

And he appeared unto them.

"What the hell are you doing here!?" screamed ULBTX-123 in his best big voice. His avatar rotated in front of them.

"We are trying to save your experiment, dumb-ass," said Gregory. "Those Planet One-"

"You don't have to tell me what Planet One has done, smallfoot! I saw it happen! I detected their beam! Now I'm trying to decide how best to destroy them once and for all."

"Oh, you don't want to do that," said Dluhosh. "And hey, haven't you grown since we last had the pleasure?"

"Yeah," said Michael. "Your legs have definitely grown longer. You'll have feet very soon at this rate."

"Really, you can tell? I mean, there are new Pixels being added all the time, but surely you can't really tell. Right?"

"Oh no, dude, you're even starting to grow a chin. I wish the bottom of my chin was that strong," said Gregory.

"My avatar is looking pretty sharp, isn't he? I was actually thinking that The Great Hologram's pecs have bulked up some too. And the Pixels in the ABDOM Region seem to have tightened up considerably. I think The Great Hologram is starting to get a six-pack. What do you think?"

The guys waited until the avatar spun back to facing them.

"Oh, man… I think you're right. Look at that, guys," said Michael.

Gregory said, "The rest of your bits seem as impressive as ever too. Your feet are going to be like cosmic canoes."

"Thank you. BUT, again, what the hell are you doing? And have you touched anything? This melted mountain has already complicated things so much, on top of everything else…" said ULBTX-123, his big voice trailing off.

"Nope, I haven't touched a thing," lied Dluhosh. "And I've only just picked up these two guys. They had no idea what was going on until just a few moments ago. So relax. You got rid of the enemy. Nice work, by the way."

"Yeah, way to keep an eye out!" said Gregory.

Dluhosh continued. "Yes, I think you are safe. From what I've seen on TV, the Earthlings' leading hypothesis involves a secret society of ape-men, or something. They have no idea. Besides, one melted mountain isn't going to change anyone's foot size."

"But how do I know it's over? What if more ships are coming? I must punish them! Destroy them!"

"I can absolutely guarantee you that they are done. They have a long history of pulling this maneuver. One ship, one mountain, and done – if it fails they know not to try again," said Dluhosh. "You snuffed them out once and for all. Good on ya!"

"Besides, if you blow up Planet One, wouldn't that alert the other Pixel People?" asked Gregory. "You won't ever be able to publish another paper."

"Hush, small-footed one! What do you know!? You pester me! I'm going to go find an asteroid big enough to take care of you! There, I'm back with an asteroid. Can you see it?"

A small asteroid appeared outside the ship's viewing dome.

"That looks like it would do the trick," said Dluhosh. "But everything will be fine if you listen to me."

"EVERYTHING is going to be fine? You don't know the half of it. I was unable to secure grant funding to continue my work. Those fool chancellors know nothing! They claimed I had created too many space-time anomalies. They actually said that this region of space is in danger of collapse. I have to scrub this whole sector and then submit to an on-site inspection as a condition of my tenure."

"An on-site inspection, eh?" said Michael. "Then you definitely don't want any missing planets…"

"Hooves! It's time that I give Planet One the hooves they deserve!"

"Alright. That sounds like a good compromise," said Dluhosh. "But just the humanoids with the striped fur, pointy ears and little button noses – everyone else is innocent."

"Should I give them cloven hooves? Or how about some heavy clompers…?"

"Cloven," said Gregory.

"I think you should go with clompers," said Michael. "Like those big horses with the hairy ankles."

Dluhosh asked, "By the way, may I ask what you did to the mountain melting battleship and crew?"

"I fed them to my dinosaurs, of course."

"Oh wow, that must have been a sight," said Michael.

"It was taking too long to unfold, so I didn't get to watch. My dinosaurs are tricky and cunning. They are saving the crew for something big – a big feast. I left because I have to guard Earth and scrub all this stupid space. But rest assured – it will not end well for them."

"Um, ULBTX-123?" said Dluhosh in a much sweeter tone than he'd used the last time he made this request. "Dnooblia, please… Can you take me there now?"

"NO! Do you not listen, silly ammonite? I just told you that I have to scrub space-time wrinkles. I'm certainly not going to create another wrinkle for you and these insolent small-foots. I suggest you get moving before I scrub away all the wrinkles you need to get you home. Now go!"

"Let's go!" said Miles, wagging his tail.

The galactic autotranslator had translated Miles' arf into 'Let's go!'

"Hey, that was cool!" said Gregory. "We can talk to Miles!"

"Let's go!" said Miles again.

"That's probably his favorite phrase. Like 'Let's go for walkies' you know. He knows that one," said Gregory.

Michael said, "Kitty!"

Miles said, "KILL KILL, KILL KILL… KILL… KILL, KILL KILL KILL!"

The headless, lower-leg and armless, but otherwise well-endowed, rotating naked blue avatar of ULBTX-123 disappeared.

"Oh, come on!" said Dluhosh. "It takes months to get to Dnooblia from here!"

Dluhosh became papillated, flashed a rainbow of metallic colors across his body, and flailed his tentacles in frustration dangerously close to the Earthlings.

"Damn it!" Then looking at the guys he said, "Well, he didn't make me throw you back this time anyway. You still want to go?"

"Let's go!" said all three of them.

"Okay. I hope you guys like watching Trukk-9 films. Oh, and one thing I can guarantee you – his dinosaurs will not eat the insectoids on that battleship. If anything, they will welcome them with open wings and feed them muffins. So, here's what I propose. We take care of some important business on Dnooblia, then head to Mother Roost to help with a rescue. You'll find that planet to be very interesting if you like dinosaurs. And I have a feeling that Mother Roost, through alien contamination, may have just found herself to be the newest member of the Galactic Pool. This is something that a good rogue Dnooblian would help to facilitate."

The Bee knows to sting only when the time is right.
And then it dies.
~ O'Buzznid-3

GRIFFER AND GRO SKOO PLOT

Vice President Griffer-1 sat at his desk watching some of the video collected by Dluhosh and Fleence on Earth. It was mainly footage of people blowing themselves up, but he also watched a few clips of people blowing up other people. He wasn't watching because he enjoyed it. He was just researching what kinds of mischief he could get up to if he were in control of beings such as these.

There was a knock at his office door. It was Gro Skoo's special knock.

Griffer-1 flipped down the screen on his computer and said, "Come."

Gro Skoo stepped in. He had stopped wearing business suits, and had switched to flowing embroidered robes. This robe was a shiny light-green color with silver-threaded trim. He thought the robes helped hide his girth better. He said, "Griffer, I have the report you wanted on that planet called Mother Roost."

"Oh good. Are they decent folk?"

"I'm afraid not. The PLUMBOB video shows nothing but friendly, fun-loving huge birds. The checklist was dominated by good stuff – baking, recreational sports, camping out, and even riding ocean waves on little flat boats. There was more footage of wave riding and random jumping around than there was of traffic jams or pollution. Plus, the PLUMBOB agent categorized their wave riding game as 'communing with energy', which is a very rare checklist item and will likely score them big points in the video voting process. I would suspect, for example, that the Plasmanoids of Blue-5 will vote with Mother Roost unanimously because of this."

"What kind of bad stuff did PLUMBOB find? There must be something useful," said the Vice President.

"The worst thing we have is 'cursing after a serious injury'. But it's actually some of the best cursing you'll ever hear. If that clip gets broadcast, it will probably sway young voters in favor of these people. Let's see… Other bad stuff… They have television, but they don't really watch much. They are known to over-indulge in muffins."

"So even the bad stuff is pretty good?"

"I'm afraid so."

"What do they look like?" asked Griffer-1.

"They do have that going against them. They are large, shaggy avianoids – goofy-looking and extremely noisy. In fact, I could envision Fermament-4 voting in favor of Mother Roost just to have someone uglier than themselves in the Galactic Pool."

"How would you describe them politically?"

"Filthy hippies."

"Well Gro Skoo, we um…" Griffer-1 paused two beats, and…

"Ha ha! We clearly don't want them in the Galactic Assembly."

"I suppose you are right, in principle, Skoo. Are we absolutely sure about PLUMBOB's data quality?"

Gro Skoo bit, yet again. "No. In fact, the PLUMBOB agent who led the mission went AWOL and I've had him declared dead. The law allows verification of data and a delay in the vote under certain circumstances, including the loss of an agent. I could prepare a PLUMBOB data-verification mission – have a couple of Crickets go verify, as it were, some bad stuff. It wouldn't even require you or the President to sign off on it. It would be strictly routine and could delay a vote by a year or more."

Griffer-1 affirmed the proposition with an almost imperceptible twitch of his ear. He said, "The PLUMBOB agents would, of course, need good instructions…"

"Understood. In fact, I have a couple of Crickets in mind. They have a particular zest for their job. Oh, by the way. How is your little grandbaby?"

"Not bad. At least he got the cloven hooves instead of the big hairy clompers like some of the unfortunates. He's quite the little climber."

Though they may strike you and call you fish-bait, and then give your book a one-star review, turn the other mandibular articulation.
~ O'Buzznid-3

J-FREZ AND THE PREZ

Jacques "Jimmy" Fresneaux fidgeted over some fishing tackle on his dining room table. He was nervous about today's fishing trip. Fleence-18 called from the bedroom.

"Jacques, honey? My mother is coming over with some of the girls for our morning tea and therapeutic swim. So please remove all your wormy things from the kitchen. You might as well get used to it now, honey – there will be no lures in the house after the baby comes."

Fleence walked into the room. She wore canvas maternity fatigues, but Jimmy chose to see her in a maternity Chompy Chunkbaits sponsorship jersey with vented shorts.

"But Fleence, you know who I'm fishing with this afternoon. I want to be extra well prepared. Plus I'm nervous that he's going to recognize me. Don't you think he'll recognize me?"

"Jacques, if he hasn't recognized you on TV already... Don't worry honey, maybe pull your hat down and wear some of those silly sunglasses if it makes you feel better."

"What if it's a trap?" Jimmy held out a big fistful of plastic worms as if to illustrate being in the grip of a trap.

"Honey, I think even the President is smart enough to get you without having your camera crew and all those fangirls hanging around to witness it. Now please clean this up. Mother will be here any min-"

The doorbell rang. Fleence's mother, Kyleence, let herself and several other very pregnant friends in. "YOOHOO?! We're here!"

"Oh Mother, you look like the twins are about to be born at any minute!"

"They sure kick like they're trying to escape! Big feet on these two..." Kyleence said, rubbing her big belly and looking at the piles of worms on the table, "Hello Jacques. Going fishing, are we?"

"With the President! He says he's a big fan. I had to invite him, but I didn't think he'd really accept. Do you think he knows?"

"Jacques, even if he remembers you, he'll recall it fondly. Now, Jacques, I have a friend here who I'd like to introduce you to. As you can see, she is not yet pregnant."

"Um, well, I'm kind of running late..."

"Oh, Jacques, it will only take you a minute. It will give me time to make you and the President some sandwiches," said Fleence.

***

The President arrived in a black limo saucer with a unit of four Discreet Service agents. He was decked out in J-Frez branded gear including a Stanky Shad visor,

Fresneauxlaroid Basses Glasses, and a Mega-Mouth Poppin' Minnow pullover that he had made all by himself. The President seemed as nervous as Jimmy.

"Howdy!" they said to each other.

"Mister President, welcome to Chuffed-18 and my favorite private lake! I think we are going to stick some toads today!"

The President was hip to the lingo, so he replied with, "Son, I'm in hawg heaven! With this low pressure system approaching, I think we might get some hot topwater action! It's Mega-Mouth Poppin' Minnow time!"

Neither Jimmy nor the President was aware that the forecast had high pressure building into the weekend. But it was of no consequence anyway.

"Boy howdy, Mister President! You came prepared!"

The Discrete Service agents loaded the President's gear into Jimmy's boat. The President had brought along at least one of every item for sale in the J-Frez mail order Hawg-a-log, including all three-hundred varieties of Jimmy Jams plastic worms and a case of Jimmy Juice energy drinks.

"You bet, partner! Here, I even blended my own custom plastic worm scent modeled after Mango Manglers. Check it out." The President handed Jimmy a zipper bag full of large blue paddle-tail worms. Jimmy gave it a deep huff, and then another. He recognized notes of the original Mango Manglers, but he was impressed by the unique structure, the bold bouquet, and the earthy finish of this new recipe.

"Niiiice, Mister President. What do you call them?"

"Chutney Chumps! You should add them to your line-up. I was thinking you should even place my face over the cartoon worm's face on the package."

"Will do, Mister President."

The Discrete Service guys indicated to Jimmy's production staff that they'd like to know the plan.

Jimmy's producer/director explained. "Yes, gentlemen, welcome to another production of Jimmy's Fishin' Hole. My name is Pleence-18. If possible Mister President, we hope you would do a little on-camera Q&A with Jimmy here on the dock. Then we will take the camera boats up the lake to a nice little cove and set up our camera gear. Then for the opening title shot, you and Jimmy come screaming into the cove and start casting while the boat is still settling. And we also have our key grip and grabber beam tech in a cloaked ship hovering above."

Stick.E briefly decloaked his little utility saucer and sine-waved down at the boats from the viewing dome.

"We will fish in the first location for forty-five minutes. You will catch three fish each, ending on the big one, and then you'll change clothes. We should be able to film eight episodes today. Also, Jimmy is modeling a new outboard motor housing, so we want to get lots of fast running b-roll."

"Goody! I've done some boating in my time ma'am. But this powerboat is so muscular. I can't wait to ride in it," said the President.

"Good, good… Okay, for the Q&A, I'll ask the questions off camera, and Jimmy will repeat them to you Mister President. Shall we begin?"

"You bet! Fire away," said the President.

"Why did you choose to open the new Galactic Broadcasting Company with a Jimmy's Fishin' Hole marathon?"

"Because…"

"Please, Mister President, let Jimmy repeat the question before you answer."

"Oh yeah, heh heh…"

Jimmy just stood there smiling.

"Uh, Jimmy?" asked the director.

"Oh, sorry – what was the question?"

She looked at her watch and asked the question again. "Why did you choose to open the new Galactic Broadcasting Company with a Jimmy Fresneaux marathon?"

Jimmy tried a version of the question that came out close enough for the director.

"Jimmy, I named it that because I am a man of the people. This is for them."

The director tried a question that she thought they might be able to handle. "People like fishing, huh?"

Jimmy nailed it this time.

"Jimmy, my friend, I know the people, and I think that's why I specifically wrote fishing shows into the presidential decree that expanded the Galactic Broadcasting Company. I don't recall exactly where I got the idea, but my brain just seems to work that way. Heh heh, my Vice President says that ideas sneak into my brain like mice sneaking into cheese."

"So expanding TV to such an enormous size is good then?" asked the director.

"Well, Jimmy, the decree said that there would be five-hundred channels, and at first I thought all of the channels were supposed to be fishing shows, all day every day, for some reason. So that's why we showed all those episodes at once. Later my staff came up with some other ideas and suggested that I invite Trukk-9 to produce a show. Now we get dozens of new show proposals a week and I sign them all. My second favorite show after *Jimmy's Fishin' Hole* is *Snake-Ape Night Boogie*, and I like *Crime Crab* and *Squirrel Squad* a lot too. The kids love that Trukk-9 show with the Cricketman, but it's too weird for me. Good? If giving meaning to my presidency counts as good, then boy howdy!"

***

"WOOOOOOOO! FISH ON!" yelled President Gren Wee-1 in an unconscious imitation of his new best buddy Jimmy Fresneaux.

Jimmy got the net.

The President dropped his rod tip as the lunker largemouth bass went airborne next to the boat. The huge bass threw the Mega-Mouth Poppin' Minnow like it had spat a watermelon seed.

"Crimineyǃ" yelled the President. But the big bass came back and exploded on the lure again.

"There she is! What an aggressive fish! Nice job, Mister President!" said Jimmy as he netted the hawg.

"Nice job to you, son! Heh heh, you always put me on the fish, Jimmy."

Jimmy pretended to release the bass, and Stick.E took it aboard his cloaked saucer with a grabber beam.

Stick.E asked, "Jimmy, do you guys want to catch the big one again, or should I rotate in some of the smaller bass while I refresh this one with the probaluator? The hawg seems bedraggled."

In fact, just about everyone but the President was bedraggled. His fishing trip with Jimmy was now into its third week. They had managed to tape over one-hundred episodes.

"Hey Jimmy, here's one. Heh heh… How many Crickets does it take to catch a fish?"

"I don't know, Mister President," said Jimmy, even though he thought he could guess the answer.

"Only one – if you can keep him on the hook!" The President laughed hard enough for everyone. Then he said, "I got a poem for ya. Heh heh…

A Dung Beetle moved to Bukk-9
Where he thought everything would be fine
He had a hunger pang
And here's what he sang

…heh heh."

"Sang what? Isn't there a punch line?" asked Jimmy.

"Jimmy, try to keep up, son. I gave you the punch line about ten minutes ago. You just gotta match 'em up. It's much funnier that way."

"Oh, well, I'm sure it is, Mister President, sorry."

"Don't be sorry son, just try harder. Okay, here's one. Heh heh… A Cockroach, a Flea and a Dung Beetle go into a bar. The barkeep says, 'Which one of you guys brought in that churdle?' Heh heh…"

"Uh, I MIGHT get that one. I mean, I can kind of see where it's going. Is it the same punch line as I'm supposed to use for the poem?"

"No, of course not. Sheesh, Jimmy, did your mama drop you on your noggin? The punch line will come around eventually. Just pay attention."

Jimmy's phone buzzed in his pocket. It was Fleence, so he answered. "Howdy, honey! The President just caught a trophy bass, but he let it go like the true sportsman that he is."

"I'm sure he did," replied Fleence. "Jacques, when are you coming home? The baby, Jacques, you'll be here for the baby…? Isn't there some way you can – I don't know – distract the President somehow? Anyway, Jacques, you have a special visitor. You'll never guess who…"

"Dluhosh?" guessed Jimmy.

"Nope. It's Dee! And he brought kittens! They are soooo cute. Anyway, he's here visiting Trukk-9, and he was hoping he could meet the President."

"I'll ask. Hold on. Mister President, I have a friend visiting and he'd very much like to meet you. His name is Dee. He is the Bearman who grows the kittens on Free-15."

"Well sure, son. I'm a man of the people! I'm always here for them – especially if they are friends of yours with big businesses. Is he coming out fishing?"

"I'll ask. Honey, does Dee want to come out fishing with us right now?"

"I'll ask. Dee, can you go fishing right now? Uh huh… uh huh… Okay, honey, he doesn't need a license, does he?"

"Nope, just send him on out."

"Dee wants to call Stick.E to come and get him. Is that okay?" said Fleence.

"I'm sure he'd be happy to."

"Have him bring some sandwiches," said the President.

"Wait, honey, the President wants to know if you can send some sandwiches out with Dee."

"Some toaster pastries too – the cinnamon ones!" said the President.

"Did you hear that, honey? Okay, okay… Alright, we'll be waiting. Love you, honey. Wait, what?"

Fleence whispered. "The sandwich with the little note on the wrapper will be yours. Make sure the President gets the other one. Bye."

"Okay Mister President, my friend with the sandwiches will be here shortly."

"Good. Okay here's one. Heh heh… What do you get when you cross a Cricket with a Cockroach?"

"I don't know, Mister President. What do you get?"

"You'll figure it out, Jimmy. This one is an exercise to help you sharpen your wit."

The President took a cast, but came up empty. "Huh, not even a bite…" He cast again and worked the Mega-

Mouth Poppin' Minnow to the best of his ability. "What's wrong? Hey, how come you aren't fishing Jimmy?"

"Oh, sir, I just have to organize these worms. The bite will turn back on soon."

Stick.E returned and Dee appeared to fly down from the sky. He made a soft landing in Jimmy's boat.

"Hello, Mister President!" said Dee as he hugged Gren Wee-1. Then he handed a little cardboard box with holes in it to the President. "Mister President, I'd like to present you with a kitten. He's from a special line I call President Gren Meow-1. He's top-quality and a limited edition. Doesn't he look smart!"

The President popped open the lid. "Well, I'll be! He sure is a handsome fellow!" said the President.

Sure enough, the kitten looked just like the President – complete with lopsided ears and a blank expression. The President closed the box and threw it to a Discreet Service agent in the camera boat. "Here's another president for you to guard, guy! Don't let him get assassinated."

Dee turned and hugged Jimmy, then whispered in his ear. "The top sandwich is yours."

Jimmy took the sandwich out of the bag and saw that Dee had written on the wrapper: DOES HE REMEMBER??? Jimmy unwrapped the sandwich, crumpled up the paper as tight as he could, and while taking a bite he ever so slightly shook his head 'no'.

Dee waited for the President to reel in his line and then handed him the bag with the other sandwich and a pastry in it.

"Thanks! Oh look, it says 'HIYA CUTIE!' on the wrapper. I guess I have a secret admirer! So what can I do you for, son?" the President asked Dee.

"Sir, I have teenagers, and I was hoping you could help them find summer jobs, or maybe internships or something.

We are on a summer road trip, and Chuffed-18 was our first stop. The kids are working as extras on Trukk-9's new show, but I'm not sure what to do next, and being cooped up in a ship with teenagers… They are very energetic and industrious, sir."

"I appreciate energetic and industrious teenagers, Dee. I was an industrious and energetic teen myself. But I don't know. I haven't exactly been paying a lot of attention to my government since I took over the TV network. Griffer's been handling everything. So how many teens we talkin'?"

"A hundred and fourteen."

"Yikes! You Bear fellas are productive!" said the President.

"Um, yes, we can be quite fecund."

"Wait, I have an idea! Wow, this feels good. Oh boy, this might be the best idea I've had since I gave Jimmy his fishing show. You see, I have about a hundred-and-something agencies in my government. Maybe your kids could sort of act as helpers for me to stay in touch better."

"Like some kind of liaisons?" asked Dee.

"I don't know. Nothing fancy. But maybe they could visit with staff at all my agencies and write little reports on their latest doings. And they could draw pictures of their adventures. Then there'd be something for my Presidential Travelling Secretary to do too. She could supervise them and gather their reports for me. Hot damn! Then I could fish without worrying that my government was spinning out of control without me hearing about it!"

"That's a lot of responsibility, Mister President. But the kids are, uh, naturals for that kind of work," said Dee.

"Okay then, it's settled. My Presidential Travelling Secretary is sleeping in her box back at my suite. I'll call the Discreet Service goons and authorize you to wake her up.

Be careful though – she can really flip out if you open that box when she doesn't expect it."

"I'll be careful. By the way, sir, do you happen to know where the galactic autotranslator is located?"

"That's one of those so-called need-to-know things that Griffer's always talking about." The President switched to his impersonation of Griffer-1. From the side of his mouth he said, "Mister President, you don't need to know… I love it when he says that!"

"So not even a clue, Mister President? Do you know what planet it's on? Maybe you've seen pictures of it – can describe the landscape perhaps."

"Why so interested in the galactic autotranslator, son?"

"Sir, I hate that thing. It's always playing me for a fool – making up stuff I never said. It gets me in trouble all the time."

"I know what you mean. Did you see my inauguration speech when I pledged to add a new planet to the Galactic Pool?"

Before Dee could make up a fib, the President continued.

"I meant to say 'I'll sail the Galactic Pool like she was my yacht, the Miss Botanist Cay. I'll scan the horizon seeking new planetary life to plant in our verdant pasture!' Sounds good, huh?"

"That's very poetic, Mister President," said Dee.

"But, I thought Miss Botanist Cay was some famous lady. It turns out that Botanist Cay is an island somewhere. They just named my boat after that place. There is no actual lady person. Follow me, son?"

"Yes..."

"So, thanks to the confusion of that damn galactic autotranslator, my government hired a bunch of botanists, and now my office is full of all kinds of flowers and shrubs that I have to water. That's what my Presidential Travelling Secretary explained to me, anyway."

"Sounds pretty typical," said Dee.

"Yeah, so I hate the thing too," said the President. "And come to think of it, that damn autotranslator is probably why Jimmy doesn't get my jokes. So, son, what do you plan to do if you find it?"

"Trukk-9 promised me we'd make a film about the quest. The climax will be when we find it and I take a dump on it. That's all."

"What a great idea! You can make a whole series. Yes, every week you could pick a new target! But just to be clear, we're talking about just a cosmetic blemish, right? You wouldn't destroy the thing…?"

"That's right. I'm sure the thing is built to last. It would just be symbolic."

"All I can really say is that if anyone knows where that cursed device is, it would be a Cricket. Have my new interns ask around maybe."

"Thanks so much, Mister President. That's a start anyway. And when I finally fulfill my destiny, I'll be sure to hit that sucker with my best sh-"

Dee was interrupted by Jimmy's groans as he convulsed with stomach cramps. He had to be taken aboard Stick.E's ship to have his food poisoning treated. And the President promised to be back the next morning.

All who are lost should stop wandering.
~ O'Buzznid-3

YEP, CASTAWAYS

Sunlight came through the viewing dome and Captain Spotty said, "Well men, I guess I promised to visit our friends on shore if we were still here in the morning. Doc and I will pay them a brief visit and carry out diplomatic protocols. You will rest-up now so that we can continue efforts to solve our little predicament. I want each of you to continue thinking of ways to solve our technical problems, and do not hesitate to suggest even the most unlikely solution. As far as I am concerned though, we are still on a mountain-melting diplomatic mission and have no business interacting with this planet or its people. Understood?"

The men said their yes-sirs and then looked out to see smoke rising from a fresh campfire on the beach. Eleven large avianoids faced the floating saucer, waving their wings and jumping up and down. One of them was jumping considerably higher than the others.

The doctor said, "It looks as though he is enjoying his new legs. What do you think, Captain?"

"Exoskeleton, I think you and I should go ashore. I did promise a visit. Third Technician, I need you to man the grabber beams and egocite, and to keep an eye on the doctor and me while we are on shore. All other crew will get some rest. Ready Doctor?"

"Yes. Maybe you should wear the charm that Mister Dayv gave you."

Captain Spotty put the lanyard over his head and the Moth technician grabber-beamed them to shore.

They were greeted by raucous honking.

Dayv said, "Have a muffin!"

One of the other surfers produced a plank holding a couple of still-warm breakfast muffins.

"No ants in these ones, daddy-o's! Just good old-fashioned millet flour, bronto suet, nectar sugar, and love," said Dayv.

Captain Spotty and Doctor Exoskeleton graciously accepted the gift of muffins. They glanced at each other to see whether the other one would take a bite, as protocol probably dictated they should. They both shrugged and bit.

"Mister Dayv, this muffin is delicious," said Captain Spotty as he took a much larger second bite.

"I second that," said the doctor through mandibles full of muffin.

"Good stuff, huh!? We made enough extra for your whole crew, just in case. Bring them on over Cap'n, while breakfast is still warm."

"Ah, yes, but my men have been up all night trying to fix the ship. They have been ordered to rest."

Dayv said, "I guess every hombre has his own definition of what rest is, Cap'n." He pointed out to the ship.

Captain Spotty sighed when he saw the little silhouettes of his crew members lined up in front of the viewing dome.

"Seems like those cats want a little shore leave, Cap'n."

Doctor Exoskeleton said, "But I would describe the behavior as clinically restful, per your orders, Captain."

"We appreciate the hospitality, Mister Dayv. But, by law, my men are not permitted off-ship on an alien world. We are here to thank you, but we must return to the ship and continue with repairs. I wish you a good day, Mister Dayv."

The doctor said, "Captain Spotty, might I suggest that we complete an area study while we are ashore. I want to look for health and safety issues. Just in case…"

"Exoskeleton…"

"Captain, as Chief Medical Officer, I insist that I be fully prepared to protect the health of your crew. It is my duty to carry out this area study."

Captain Spotty wanted to protest, but he knew there was no use. His old friend was going to push his buttons until he got his way, so he said, "Mister Dayv, will you entertain my Chief Medical Officer's order?"

"That's direct from the fridge, Cap'n! I mean that's cool – it's super alright with me, is what I'm layin' down. Now, how can I help, Doc?" asked Dayv.

"Basically, we just need an escort to show us the important items from the health and safety checklist, and to answer a few questions."

Dayv pointed at the surfer with the new legs and said, "You stay with me, Blood. The rest of you cats get out there on dawn patrol! Don't be wasting this tide."

The rest of the surfers honked it up and ran to grab their boards.

"Okay, Cap'n, I think the best way to do this is for you cats to ride on us cats' backs."

"Like you are churdles?" asked Doctor Exoskeleton.

"Perhaps. Looks like you cats have natural grippers – just don't even think about using those spurs though, Cap'n. If you try to walk, you two'll be buried in the groundcover vegetation down there. We have a sport called dinoback riding. Blood and I are good at it. Come on, saddle up!"

The two insectoids climbed on. They found that the big avianoids pope's noses were perfect little saddles, and their erect tail feathers made for comfortable backrests. They turned and trekked toward the forest edge. A mixed flock of twittery little avianoids flew ahead of them, working both the forest and dune vegetation for their breakfasts. Small bipedal reptiloids scampered off into the groundcover ahead of them. Everything was green and alive with sound. Strange flowers, like nothing these insectoids had ever seen, peeked out through the infrequent gaps in the forest greenery.

"The odor is overwhelming. Exoskeleton, do you recognize it?"

"Oh, sorry cats, there must be a bronto nearby," said Dayv.

"No, not that Mister Dayv. I mean the fragrance of the forest – the mildew and the duff. It takes me back to a place…" Captain Spotty couldn't finish.

"Do you mean the old country before the war, Spotty?"

"Yes, Exoskeleton, that is it exactly. I suppose there are not many of us left who recall that smell of home. It is difficult to describe… Like the smell of security or the smell of laughter. I mean it, Exoskeleton. It smells happy and pure."

"I, too, think it is a lovely odor, Spotty. They say that olfaction can be a very evocative sensory perception. Your strong reaction does not surprise me."

"Oops, cats. Yep, there's a bronto nearby. Look at that – and be very careful not to let one of those hillocks drop on you."

Ahead of them just at the dune/forest interface, lay a great big pile of steaming poo. It was very much like churdle poo with lots of vegetation and fibers binding together a dozen or so 'apples' – each apple was half as big as Captain Spotty himself.

"My word!" said Captain Spotty. "That would feed the navigator and his family for a week!"

"Those big ol' Clydes are plenty docile, but they have a habit of…"

Before Dayv could finish, a head the size of a cargo transport pod crashed through the trees and stopped just short of getting Doctor Exoskeleton's face stuck in its eyeball.

"Blood, take a step back, daddy-o! That bronto must be quite frightening to your rider!"

The Doctor instinctively snapped his mandibles at the colossal beast.

"Yeah, Doc, those brontos are kinda curious about things, but they are only harmful if they DON'T see you. There's no need to tell you to keep your corpus from getting under one though, right?" said Dayv.

"I did not know the galaxy contained land beasts so large. Astonishing."

"And yummy! If one dies we scavenge the fat. It makes a superior suet. We have an old saying. Bronto wasn't bluffin' – he died for your muffin. How you cats feel?"

"Exoskeleton, is it just me, or do you feel, I do not know, energized?"

"I am experiencing the same phenomenon, Captain. I believe it may be related to the food we have eaten, or perhaps it is just exhilaration from this unusual experience. Spotty, when was the last time you ate food that didn't come from a duplicator?"

"When I was a young man on ZZZZZZ-3."

"And I have never in my life eaten anything with ingredients that did not originate in a duplicator, Spotty... Mister Dayv, what other kinds of natural hazards are there here – things such as poisonous plants and the like that we insectoids should be aware of?"

"Ah, yes – now how do I put this delicately? About the worst thing you're gonna find is a big ol' ant. Relatively big that is, Doc. Sometimes there are scads of 'em. They can put the high hurts on a guy with the big chomps they have. They aren't edible, and unfortunately, they seem to like my cabin. How about if we head on up there and I'll show you around?"

"Doctor?" said Captain Spotty.

"Yes, I believe we can safely leave sight of the ship to continue this area study. So far, so good, as we say. However, Mister Dayv and Mister Blood, we may lose our egocite vapor feed and not be able to communicate with you."

"As WE say, Doc, the country speaks for itself," said Dayv.

So up the trail they climbed. Doctor Exoskeleton noticed the forest change from one dominant tree species to another, only a short distance from the shore.

"I cannot get over the smell, Exoskeleton. Up here it is slightly different, but still has that certain something. It smells so alive. I think it is the plants. Not just one kind, but the whole mix of them. My sister works for the President now – Travelling Secretary – one of the few of us left from the old country. Anyway, she collects plants, including rare surviving black-market species from ZZZZZZ-3, and somehow she got a grant to hire collectors. She said the plants improved the atmosphere of her office. I thought she meant the overall ambiance of the place. But she may have literally meant the air. She would love this planet."

"Captain, that gives me an idea that could help boost the men's morale. You might consider collecting a few live plants with the intention of making them a gift to your sister when we return. It might help show your optimism, and, who knows, it might improve the atmosphere of the ship."

They entered into a meadow area and saw Dayv's cabin and the surfers' hovercrafts. Most of the hovercrafts had one form or another of flotation platform leaning against it or tied to the back. About every other hovercraft had a tent or lean-to next to it. And each one radiated spokes of trails to various places – Dayv's cabin, the communal latrine, the surf beach, and each neighboring hovercraft. The hovercrafts had clearly been parked there for a long time.

They did a lap around the meadow, had a peek inside the cabin, looked under the hood of Dayv's classic hovercraft, examined the vegetable garden, and marveled at the patrolling dragonflies.

***

Captain Spotty signaled for the Moth technician to grabber-beam them back to the ship. He and Doctor Exoskeleton arrived with a tray of muffins and some potted plants that the surfers had helped them collect.

"Men, while I must insist that we obey the law and remain onboard the ship, there is no reason that a few things from their world cannot come into our world. Doc has cleared these muffins, and we have both tested them. It may be weird for some of you to eat natural food – especially considering the alien source – but these muffins are a cultural experience unto themselves. As the Roostians would say, 'Have a muffin."

The men, except for one, dug in. The navigator would get his later.

"And I have brought back a few of their fragrant plants. I want to take them to my sister for her collection, so do not eat them. I assume that you are all rested and ready to finish solving our little problem."

***

After another unsuccessful night of problem solving, the crew stood looking out the viewing dome at the morning as it unfolded outside. The sunrise was an intense red, like nothing the men had ever seen.

Captain Spotty stood with his men. "This quality of light…" was all he said.

"Captain, sir, I believe one of them is signaling us," said the pilot.

"Oh, I am sure they think we need muffins. But I explained the situation. They will figure it out."

Dayv continued to jump up and down. The rest of the surfers joined him.

"Captain, they express an urgency greater than muffins," said Doctor Exoskeleton.

Then Dayv grabbed his longboard and began paddling out toward the ship.

"Oh boy. Pilot, go ahead and grabber-beam him onboard."

The pilot placed Dayv and his board into the sickbay. "Cap'n and Doc, yo cats, look I gotta lay something on you. We have a saying that goes, 'Red sky in morning, go find some shelter.' So me and the cats are gonna head back to civilization until it blows over. But I have to ask, Cap'n, how are you anchored? Because it's gonna maybe get real bumpy and blowy out here."

"Yes, that is a concern, Mister Dayv. We have grabber beam piles supporting us, but they are only as strong as the material they grab," said Captain Spotty. "Our closed hull, however, is unsinkable and impact resistant. I suspect we will be fine."

"Well I suspect you ought to come back to town with us, Cap'n. We can hide you in our board bags, no problem."

I am sorry, Mister Dayv. While we greatly appreciate your offer, it is not an option for us."

"Okay, Cap'n, I understand, I guess. I'll be back to check on you first thing if the roads are open. But you have to promise an evening campfire session with the crew when the storm blows over."

"I am sorry, Mister Dayv, but a jamdown is also not an option. We will look forward to your return, however. Thank you."

***

The ship was not immune to the forces of nature. The storm had overwhelmed the ship's moorings and it was creeping closer to shore. The hull was now contacting the bottom of the sea as the storm waves rolled past and the ship dipped into the troughs.

"CREW REPORT!"

"Captain, the Moths are still very seasick, but everyone else is secure," said Doctor Exoskeleton.

"Engineering!"

"She is holding together, sir, but I do not know how much more banging she can take! The outer hull is taking a severe beating!" said the Bee, with a hand-held scanner in one tarsus and a roll of tape in the other. He was hunkered down in his honeycomb. And everyone else was hunkered too, each in his own way – except for Captain Spotty.

He had relieved the sick Moths on grabber beam duty. But as he predicted, it wasn't a question of the strength of the grabber beams or the skill of the operator. The problem was the questionable integrity of the substrate.

The seabed beneath them was sand and gravel, but the grabber beams could only dig deep enough to enclose relatively small sandbag-like bundles, which the ship dragged along the bottom. Captain Spotty saw the seastack out on the point during flashes of lightning. He attempted to grab at the seastack, but only succeeded in breaking away chunks of rock. The seastack was far too large and distant to completely encase, even with the super grabber on full power. He tried pushing off the land in front of them, but the giant waves and hurricane-force winds moved the mass of the ship with much more power than the grabber beams could push against.

To keep himself alert, Captain Spotty sang space shanties.

"Was you ever down on Planet One?" sang the captain.
"Was you ever down on Planet One?" repeated the crew.
"Wishin' that you had a gun!"
"Wishin' that you had a gun!"

"Was you ever down on Bounty-2?"
"Was you ever down on Bounty-2?"
"While we wondered where was you!"
"While we wondered where was you!"

"Was you ever up on ZZZZZZ-3?"
"Was you ever up on ZZZZZZ-3?"
"There is naught left to please a Flea!"
"There is naught left to please a Flea!"

"Was you ever down on Fermament-4?"
"Was you ever down on Fermament-4?"
"Wishin' you could find the door!"
"Wishin' you could find the door!"

Captain Spotty rubbed his wings together and led his crew in space shanties through the night, and he knew a lot of them, including at least fifteen different things you would or would not want to have happen when you were either up or down on all eighteen planets of the Galactic Pool. His shanty for Swampy-12 was too rude for print, per the decency standards of the Galactic Pool Publishing Agency.

The Click Beetle pilot kept a simple rhythm going until he was exhausted. Captain Spotty ran out of songs. And the engineer said, "I do not know how much more she can take..."

***

The morning came. The storm continued to blow. But the peak winds had passed and the storm surge had subsided. The ship still rocked when the largest sets of breakers reached it. The men looked toward shore. They'd suffered no casualties, and the Moths were over their seasickness. The storm surge and swells had combined to push the Battleship Aedeagus up the shore and well into the dunes, where its leading edge had been knocking down a grove of tall thin trees.

Captain Spotty addressed his crew. "The ship is apparently no worse-off than before the storm. I appreciate your fortitude through the night, even if your space shanties could use some improvement. Take the day off. Get caught up on your letters home. Dismissed."

All of the men stayed on the bridge to watch the storm.

After the tide and swell had dropped, and the surf no longer rocked the ship, a bronto poked its head out from behind the line of fallen trees. It stretched its neck out and licked the ship's viewing dome in front of the crew. Its head continued to investigate until it was apparently satisfied with whatever it thought the ship was.

Then the pilot said, "Hey, is that Dayv up there?"

The crew could see Dayv and a couple of the surfers jumping and flapping yet again. Captain Spotty had learned not to ignore their jumping and flapping. The surf still ran up the beach too far to allow them to make it to the ship. So Captain Spotty ordered the pilot to grabber-beam them over.

Dayv, 'Blood', and a couple of others stood wet and muddy on the bridge.

"Cap'n, Cap'n, the bridge is out... There's an orphanage... Collapsed..." said Dayv as he panted from the exertion of running all the way from the washed out bridge.

"Why? Why does it always have to be the orphanages? Those poor kids. Is it bad?" asked Captain Spotty.

"Real bad, Cap'n. The building collapsed. They would have been sheltering in the basement, and now they are trapped."

"Injuries?" asked Doctor Exoskeleton.

"We don't know. Could be a lot if they weren't in the basement. And there's still a chance of the basement flooding."

Captain Spotty said, "We wish we could help, Mister Dayv."

"Wish? Well, I grant your wish, Cap'n. Let's go! We need your doctor. And do you have one of those loader beam doohickeys that could go there?"

"You do not understand, Mister Dayv. I am forbidden from interfering. The penalties are harsh."

"Cap'n, you have accepted our hospitality – you wear the tooth of the plesiosaur – you have eaten the muffins. Cap'n, you are one of us. Do you mean to tell me that you would be forbidden from helping your own?"

Captain Spotty kicked at the corner of the carpet as he thought. "Mister Dayv, yes, I would be forbidden from helping even Crickets."

Doctor Exoskeleton said, "However, Captain, you would be REQUIRED to rescue them if they were somehow Planet One humanoids."

"Doctor, come with me," said Captain Spotty.

They went into the Captain's prep room. "Doctor, do you believe that there are times when a law is clearly unjust, and MUST be disobeyed?"

"Of course I do. I am a Doctor, Spotty. I have a trump law. Now, I do not want to play the Doctor Card in front of the crew again. But I will. You know I will."

They went back out to the ship's bridge where Dayv was already sketching a diagram of the orphanage for the crew. Captain Spotty said, "Okay men, each of you grab a portable grabber beam unit. Doctor, bring your field kit. Moths, you stay here. Give Dayv and his guys a concentrated dose of egocite vapor and put a thousand-PSI canister on a backpack frame. As soon as we are equipped, place us up the trail as far as you can."

"Wicked, Cap'n! I knew you were a real man."

The second technician Moth placed them on the trail above the pounding surf.

Dayv said, "It's a good five clicks to the river, Cap'n. You all should ride on us as we run. Just hold your gear. It might be a bit slow, but we'll get there."

"I think my men are capable of flying there, right boys?"

"Yessir!"

"Good, Doctor Exoskeleton and I will ride. The rest of you take the gear on ahead and assess the situation."

The Bee engineer was first to arrive at the washed-out bridge. Even with a full-on super grabber, there was nothing that could have been done to fix the shattered timbers. The Click Beetle pilot and Dung Beetle navigator arrived next.

"How did Dayv and the guys even get across this?" asked the pilot.

Dayv and 'Blood' ran up with Captain Spotty and Doctor Exoskeleton riding like experts in their tail-feather saddles. They looked at the raging brown river below. They watched a large tree float by.

"I dare say it's even risen a little since we came across," said Dayv.

"How did you…?"

"We jumped, Cap'n. 'Blood' almost made it the whole way. The rest of us were able to glide far enough to clear the water and then climb up the bank."

"Impressive. It should be a simpler matter with these grabber beams. Okay, men, let us get everyone across safely. And Dayv, if possible, I would like to minimize the number of people who see us. Hopefully we will be able to move the rubble and go unseen by the orphans. We will figure out how to disguise the doctor if needed."

"He can wear my poncho, Cap'n. Should cover him like a tent."

***

They all jumped into the waiting hovercrafts with the gear and zoomed off to the orphanage.

The surfers who had remained were removing rubble from near where the entrance used to be, but they hadn't made any progress to speak of.

The ship's crew got to work. First they moved the orphanage's staff's hovercrafts. Then they used the grabber beams to pull the rubble as instructed by the Bee engineer. No chunk of rubble was too large for the skilled manipulation of the grabber beams by Captain Spotty's crew. Before long they had tossed a rather large pile of rubble over the orphanage's hedge, all while keeping the remaining rubble stable.

"I think I hear something," called out the Click Beetle, his head in a hole with antennae extended through gaps in the debris.

The Bee engineer assessed the debris pile. He ordered the removal of a large concrete slab, which took four grabber beams to move.

"Cap'n, I think we have access to the cellar through this gap. Should we go in, or try to widen it some more for Mister Dayv's men? Could take a few minutes."

Captain Spotty looked at Dayv and the Doctor. "Pilot, are you comfortable going in?"

"Yessir!"

"Make it happen."

The Click Beetle pilot took a light and disappeared down the hole. Everyone else gathered around the opening – on edge and ready to respond to the slightest movement of debris.

After several nervous minutes, the Click Beetle popped up and handed Dayv a cute little fuzzy flightless bird with a long beak. "This is the orphan making the noise. The rest of the place is empty. He's the only one."

Dayv took the small animal from the Click Beetle and said, "That's no orphan – well maybe he is – but this is just a stray pee-wee bird." Then he started laughing.

The rest of the guys joined him.

Blood said, "Dayv, they must have evacuated ahead of the storm. No wonder we were the only ones who stopped to help, big cat. The teachers must have left their hovercrafts and went on a hoverbus with the orphans, or something."

"Um, sorry Cap'n. I guess me and the cats freaked out a little bit there."

Everyone enjoyed a hearty laugh and a good honking. They spent the rest of the afternoon clearing rubble to at least give the orphanage a head start on getting rebuilt. The outdoor work was a treat for the crew as well. The pee-wee bird stuck around and begged some day-old muffin crumbs from the surfers.

"I'm going to continue back to my cabin if you'll give me a lift over the ravine, Cap'n. A few of the cats will be back when things dry out a bit. Then we'll have that – what did you call it? A campfire what?"

"A campfire jamdown, Mister Dayv... A campfire jamdown."

Cultural change is not a step in cheese making.
~ O'Buzznid-3

BACK ON DNOOBLIA

Dluhosh piloted his cloaked ship through the final wormhole on his route back to Dnooblia. He verified that the wormhole pointed in the general direction of Earth. It occurred to him that this wormhole was probably the one that ULBTX-123 had created when he'd brought Dluhosh's ancestors from Earth all those millions of years ago.

This was Dluhosh's first trip home in almost three years. He had so much that he wanted to do, and so many people he wanted to see, and he held the answer to the question of the ages. But a rookie rogue Dnooblian would be wise to be extra careful. And Dluhosh was wise. Keep it quick and simple, he thought.

"Okay guys," he said to Michael, Gregory and Miles. "I've been thinking hard about this for the past few weeks. I need to stay off the radar screen, literally and figuratively. But I want to see my friend Mudhosh. It sounds like he needs help – if it's not too late. I may want to invite him to go with us, but only if he's passed the humanoid tolerance test, of course."

"Um, yeah, that would be a good idea, you know," said Gregory.

"Right, but I just want to be careful. I won't put you in harm's way, and we need to make it quick."

"Okay, but don't be TOO careful and quick. This is pretty exciting for us. We'd kind of like to do Dnooblia a little. You know, go for walkies…" said Michael.

"WALKIES WALKIES WALKIES!" said Miles.

"We'll try. Anyway, that bluish dot is home. I'll zoom in. See the main continent? That's where I live – on the western coast right here." He zoomed into a peninsula sticking out into the ocean.

"It's afternoon there right now, but I want to wait until night to go see Mudhosh. Before we land – as a precaution – and this is only a precaution – I think it would be a good idea to download and save a record of your complete memories," said Dluhosh. "This could be useful in case you are overly blown away by the amazingness of Dnooblia."

"You mean like Dnooblia is so amazing that it might make us go insane? Okay, you make it sound pretty amazing with the ammonites and flying weasels and stuff, but is it really that much cooler than Earth?" asked Michael.

"Yes. Our first stop is going to be a remote beach that is usually littered with ammonite shells. And collecting is legal. That will be my welcome-to-Dnooblia gift to you before I go do what I have to do for my friend."

Dluhosh copied their memories onto the ship's computer and then they flew into the Dnooblian atmosphere.

"Do you think it would be a good idea for us to have a dose of calming agent before we arrive too? I'm kind of nervous about losing my mind and everything like you said, you know…" said Gregory.

"How DID I know…?"

So Michael and Gregory domed themselves and hit the calming agent button about a dozen times.

"Um, okay, we had three doses, so we should be… fine. I love you Dluhosh," said Michael.

"Sure, Michael – whatever you say."

"No man, seriously, you're the best."

"Yeah, dude, he's right. You are awesome. You've given us so much. What an opportunity…" added Gregory.

"Don't try to play me, guys. How many doses did you just have?"

Tears welled up in Michael's eyes.

"Uh, maybe four, I think…" said Gregory. "But look – now you've hurt Michael's feelings."

Dluhosh set the guys and Miles down on the beach of a beautiful little uninhabited tropical island with white coral sand and a fringing reef. They had themselves a shell collecting orgy, and Dluhosh let them do some diving with a Grabber Beam Underwater Breathing Apparatus (GBUBA). It was, without a doubt, the highlight of both their lives by about a million times. They couldn't be sure, but they thought it was probably better than sex.

***

Dluhosh landed his ship on Mudhosh's lawn. It was just after dark. A light was on inside the house.

"Here's the plan. I think it would be best to meet him in his house where he'll be most comfortable. So you guys stay here and watch from the port. Assuming everything is fine, I'll come out and give you the signal. Descend from the ship one at a time, and don't make eye contact with Mudhosh until he greets you."

"Should we maybe have a dose of calming agent?" asked Gregory. "I'm still all jittery from finding all these shells. Look at this! Yeah, we need to calm down."

Dluhosh didn't bother to reply. As soon as he left the ship though, the guys domed themselves again.

Dluhosh climbed down, flattened himself into a disk, and made his skin the texture and color of the grass. From the middle of the lawn he pushed the doorbell with a tentacle tip, then withdrew it in case someone other than Mudhosh answered.

"Come in…" said a weak voice.

By not immediately hiking to the door to greet his visitor, Mudhosh had violated the Rules of Terrestrial Ambulation. Dluhosh viewed this apparent transgression as confirmation of his fears for Mudhosh's wellbeing. So he opened the door just a crack, stuck his beak in, and said, "Mudhosh, is that you?"

"Yeah… My name is Mudhosh. Who else would be sitting here all alone with no fresh fish in the fridge? Who is it?"

"It's Dluhosh."

Mudhosh whipped a tentacle around the knob and yanked the door open.

"Dluhosh! Is it really you!? Oh, Dluhosh, I'm so sorry for not coming to the door. I'm so weak…" Mudhosh's skin flashed fuchsia and then switched right back to a dewy gray.

"Oh no. Do they have you on the anti-rogue meds?"

Mudhosh didn't reply to the question. Instead he said, "Dluhosh, I'm so happy to see you. I haven't been this happy since the night we got our sprinting licenses – not even close. I failed the family reliance test for three years running, and they permanently disqualified me. They said I was a maritime hazard after I jumped a shark in the shipping lanes. I love the ocean Dluhosh, but it has a weird effect on me. But a good kind of weird – not weird like these meds…"

"Did you try to go rogue, Mudhosh?"

"No Dluhosh, I don't have the mantle for that. But they judged me a high risk because I fit their stupid criteria. I've just been sitting here for months watching a TV show of a humanoid who can catch more fish than me. He's very funny, but it kind of makes me more depressed to watch him catch fish after fish when I know I can hardly catch one. But I can't stop watching."

"Mudhosh, I think I can help you. But first, answer me a question. Are you in a good enough state of mind to hear three shocking pieces of information in quick succession?"

"I don't know Dluhosh. I'm happy just to feel ANYTHING these days."

"Okay. Here goes… I'm pretty sure I've discovered the Ancestral Dnooblian."

Mudhosh flashed fuchsia again. He examined Dluhosh's skin for signs of deception. "Either you've gotten very good at poker, I've gone colorblind, or you really did find the Ancestral Dnooblian."

"I have a fossilized specimen on my ship. It's right outside."

"I didn't hear you fly in. Wait, you have a ship?"

"It's cloaked."

"Cloaked?! But only the police… or a rogue would… Dluhosh-10, you aren't messing with me are you?"

"It's just 'Dluhosh' now. Or Dluhosh-X if you need to put something on the end there."

"Dluhosh! No! Really?" Mudhosh maintained his fuchsia a little longer this time.

"Are you still alright, Mudhosh?"

"Dluhosh! You, you, you… Rogue?"

"Yes. Now are you ready for the third shocker."

"I feel good Dluhosh. I don't know why, but… Go ahead."

"Is that fishing humanoid on TV named Jimmy Fresneaux by any chance?"

"Yeah, have you been watching his show too?"

"No, I haven't been around much lately."

"Oh Dluhosh, it's almost the most popular thing on TV – J-Frez and *Dab Tabmow, ManCricket.* Dab Tabmow is Trukk-9, so of course it's brilliant, but J-Frez is just so way out there. His show is truly bizarre – been nothing like it EVER. I even ordered one of J-Frez's visors." Mudhosh grabbed his Chompy Chunkbaits visor and hooped it over the peak of his head and it twirled down to his eyes like a dying ghula ghoop. "You do know that TV has changed a lot since you've been gone, right?"

"I knew there were some plans, but I haven't been able to see. I do know Jimmy Fresneaux personally though. He's from the planet where I did my last PLUMBOB mission – the one where the Ancestral Dnooblian is from. We Dnooblians are blood relatives of Earthlings like Jimmy. We even share DNA. I helped make the pilot episode for his first show on Earth."

"What!? Nuh-uh… Don't mess around, Dluhosh. Really, you know J-Frez?! Do you think I could meet him?" Mudhosh's normal brick-red color was returning.

"Maybe one day, sure. But right now do you think you could handle seeing an Earthling humanoid like Jimmy in the flesh?"

"Dluhosh, I passed the humanoid tolerance rite a long time ago. Plus I'm so used to seeing J-Frez on TV. I'm inured. And frankly, I'm quite bored with the whole dismembering of humanoids thing. You outgrow it. You really do. Besides, I'm so weak from the meds that I doubt I could even eviscerate one right now."

"Come here. Look out on the lawn."

Mudhosh saw the outline of a humanoid standing in a free-floating doorway above the middle of his lawn. Gregory smiled and waved.

"You see that?" asked Dluhosh.

"Yeah! He looks even funnier than J-Frez! Can we invite him in?"

"Are you sure now? Seeing him isn't giving you the willies? I could bring him in with a grabber beam."

"Dluhosh… Don't you trust me?"

"Of course I trust you Mudhosh. I'm just trying to gage your comfort level."

Mudhosh held out a tentacle tip to show that it wasn't snapping. He was also keeping his color steady.

"You do seem fine…"

"Totally! But where did you get him? How did…?"

"There are two. Think you can handle two?"

"No problem! I'd love to talk to them – like have a sort of reconciliation process with the humanoids. Dluhosh, I'm probably the most humanoid-tolerant Dnooblian there is. Except for you, maybe."

Dluhosh regarded his friend. He seemed stabilized. So Dluhosh stood close, just in case, and signaled for Gregory to approach.

Gregory came down the ladder very calmly. He was so calm that he seemed to flow across the lawn. Then Michael appeared in the floating doorway. Dluhosh gave him the signal and he flowed in formation behind Gregory.

When Gregory reached the porch, he extended his hand and Mudhosh took it with his first hunting tentacle. And he did not break Gregory's fingers or yank his arm out of its socket. He asked Gregory if he'd like to have a seat and enjoy some fish wine. Gregory accepted the invitation and oozed into an easy-chair.

Michael approached in much the same way, but something happened.

Mudhosh grabbed Michael around the neck with one hunting tentacle, and Gregory around the neck with the other. Before Dluhosh could intervene, Mudhosh was spinning the guys around so fast that they were almost invisible. It was over in seconds.

"GHAAAAAA! MUDHOSH!!!!" Dluhosh formed a tent with his web to enclose his friend. Mudhosh collapsed into a lump of moist gray flesh, his beak chattering. Dluhosh looked around the room. He was unable to work out which limbs belonged to which torso. The walls and ceiling were dripping red. It was like the whole room had been turned into a blender.

"So much blood... They have so much blood..." Dluhosh vomited.

"Dluhosh? Dluhosh?" said Mudhosh from under Dluhosh's web. "We can rebuild them, right?"

"Um, well, no. Not even with a medical grade quantum duplicator. We'd have needed the buckets of blood prefabricated. Plus… Uh, their heads… Maybe the heads could have been salvaged after they hit the second or third wall. But after you smashed them into the fourth wall, it became hopeless. My god, look at this mess…"

Mudhosh crawled out from under his friend. "Oh, no. What have I done? Dluhosh, it was his smell. There was something peculiar about his odor. I think it came from his mouth. The little one seemed fine, but gheh! I'm so sorry Dluhosh. This is too much..."

"Take it easy Mudhosh. We'll just have to clean this up. Nobody here knows those guys. No one has to know."

"But Dluhosh, the nurses come to check on me every morning. We can't clean this by then."

"Well then, Mudhosh, I think you just went rogue. Welcome aboard."

Mudhosh just stared at his friend.

"Come on, let's gather up the bigger chunks. We'll preserve some samples and dispose of the rest in my matter converter."

"I don't think I'd feel right eating food from your duplicator knowing that these humanoids went into the matter converter – no desserts anyway."

"That's fine. I'm getting low on calming agent. We'll convert their remains and pump them directly into the holding tanks. It would have made them happy to be recycled that way. Come on, we have to get out of here."

The two Dnooblians sprinted to the waiting ship.

When they got on board, Miles said, "HEY HEY HEY HEY, HEY HEY HEY!"

"Whoa! Dluhosh, what's that?"

"Oh yeah, I forgot. The poor pup just lost his best friends. I'm sorry Miles."

"Dluhosh, is he sapient?"

"Not entirely, but he's pretty smart for a little animal. In fact…"

Dluhosh turned to the computer and said, "Pull up the memory files of Michael and Gregory. This just might work, Mudhosh."

"Dluhosh, are you sure it's safe? He's such a little animal compared to the humanoids."

"Yeah, I think there's plenty of room in there. I can remove all of their motor memory and sex drive triggers, for example. If I leave the vocal motor memory in, they should be able to control Miles' noises enough to trigger the galactic autotranslator. There's a lot of wasted space in their minds that they won't need in Miles. With minimal compression we should be able to preserve all three minds. Here we go."

Dluhosh hit send Michael's and Gregory's minds were uploaded into Miles' brain.

"HEY!"

"HEY!"

"HEY!"

"Okay, take it easy guys! Here's some calming agent. There you go…" said Dluhosh.

The three guys continued haying from their shared mouth.

"Sit!" said Dluhosh.

They sat, and one of them asked, "What happened? What now?"

"There was an accident. Um, a plasma leak. You do not have any memory of it, of course. I have loaded minimal versions of your minds into Miles' brain. You won't be able to control Miles' body, and he won't be able to read your minds or anything silly like that. But you should have some control of Miles' vocal apparatus. All you'll likely hear is garbled dog sounds, but the egocite vapor will allow the autotranslator to convey the exact meaning to us. We'll even see his lips move like he's actually saying your words. I hope it doesn't freak him out too much. The poor boy…"

"So we're dead, aren't we?"

"Um, death is kind of a relative state… Right? You feel alive, don't you?"

"I guess, but what do we do now?"

"I'll explain, but first, this is my friend Mudhosh."

"Hi guys."

"We've heard a lot about you, Mudhosh. So you passed the humanoid tolerance test, then?" asked Gregory from the lips of Miles.

"Oh yes, long ago..."

"Well congratulations," said Michael.

"Yeah, congrats! I know it must have been tough. I have a hard time tolerating most of them myself," said Gregory.

"Thank you. Dismembering humanoids isn't nearly as fun as you'd think. Really," replied Mudhosh.

Miles himself continued to whine. He curled up on the couch and stared at Mudhosh.

Dluhosh explained the next step. "We have to get you to Chuffed-18. They can clone you new bodies there. You can probably have your full minds uploaded as soon as the little fetuses' brains develop sufficiently. That's up to you. Also, do you want to remain in Miles' brain for the time being? Or we can just erase you from there and wait until you have a new body. Your births would be instantaneous from your perspective."

"We'd have to be born again? Oh, man. What?!"

"I'm really sorry about this, guys. We couldn't have known about the plasma leak just then. Uh, you didn't feel a thing," said Dluhosh, flashing colors that the Earthlings couldn't interpret.

"Miles seems stressed out about our voices coming out of him. Will he get used to it?" asked Gregory.

"Maybe. But if you just keep quiet, he won't know you are there. I think he'll be fine."

"Can you please feed him OUR food, you know?" suggested Gregory.

"Yeah, that would make him happier too," said Michael. "Just no beans."

"If you want him happier, I hope you like playing a lot of fetch and tug-of-war," said Dluhosh.

"Whoa, man, I can smell everything! And it all smells so good. Smells the same as it always did, but strong and good!" said Michael.

"Alright, then it's off to Chuffed-18," said Dluhosh.

"I'm going to meet J-Frez!" said Mudhosh. "And sometimes he fishes with President Gren Wee! I'm so excited. I've never left Dnooblia before. And… and, I'm rogue…"

Miles could sense Mudhosh's joy, and he wagged his tail.

***

On their way to Chuffed-18, Mudhosh was able to tune in pay-for-a-view *Dab Tabmow, ManCricket* episodes. Dluhosh was, of course, also interested in seeing the latest works of Trukk-9. So they agreed to have a Dab Tabmow marathon.

"Okay, Dluhosh, Dab Tabmow exists as the result of a failed artificial evolution experiment. He is half Cricket, and half Bukk-9 humanoid. See? He talks like a Bearman, and he is as honest as a Dnooblian. So he can't fit in anywhere. And so… And so, he walks the land eking out an honest living and helping the needy and the downtrodden. More the downtrodden… But they always find out his true identity and shun him. Okay, okay, this episode is when he… but wait… We don't know any of this until later…"

"Mudhosh! Just play it. I'll catch on. No spoilers," said Dluhosh.

Mudhosh hit play.

From high above, the image slowly zooms down on a desert landscape. Dust-devils and dry creek beds become apparent, and these are the only features save a small dark dot in the top center of the view. The dot kicks up a small dust cloud that gets sucked into a whirl-wind. The camera is now racing up behind the black-cloaked and hooded figure as the theme music builds. The music is, of course, a Dnooblian tenor singing an aria of great foreboding.

"Yeah! I love that opening, Dluhosh."

"Yep, classic Trukk-9…"

The view displays the posture and gait of the figure as the camera pivots around him in a three-sixty. He walks with a tired dignity, carrying only a water gourd, a walking stick, and a shoulder bag with a bed roll sticking out. The figure's features are cloaked in shadow, but then a bird of prey shrieks and Dab Tabmow throws his hood back. His head is a hideous blend of incongruous features: small forked antlers, a pair of serrated mandibles, compound eyes scattered seemingly at random about an armored head, and a fleshy humanoid nose. A voice-over narration begins.

"I am Dab Tabmow. I am a nomad. I am a warrior. I seek out the downtrodden misfits of this world. I hug them and make them feel better about themselves. I am Dab Tabmow."

Dab Tabmow walks on, away from the view, as the music builds again. The scene cuts to Dab Tabmow approaching the gates of a small city. He reads in voice-over from a poster that is nailed to the city wall.

"Tournament today! All comers! All superpowers welcome! Three PM! Feast for the winner!"

A deep rumbling sound builds in the background until it becomes a full clap of thunder. It is the trademarked Dab Tabmow hunger pang, from which his Multi-Vision Tornado Attack power emanates.

Dab Tabmow glances up at the sun and pokes a short stick into the ground. In tight close-up he squints all ten of his functioning eyes.

"Two fifty-nine!" he shouts as he twists into tornado form and streaks through the city gates.

The scene cuts to Dab Tabmow as he faces his final opponent of the tournament. In voice-over he says, "You are worthy, young mutant. But I am hungrier. Please don't do anything silly and make me hurt you, buddy."

"Dab Tabmow, you are known, but of the unknown. I am honored to engage you in combat. May each of us learn something valuable from this conflict!"

They lunge at each other. The young mutant lands three rapid hand-kicks and three more foot-punches. Dab Tabmow reels. The young mutant jumps high overhead and spins his varied appendages into a single buzz-saw. Dab Tabmow shouts, "MULTI-VISION TORNADO ATTACK, LEVEL FIVE!" as he blurs into a stout tornado spinning in the opposite direction of the young mutant buzz-saw falling toward him. As the opposite-spinning forces encounter one another, sprites of golden plasma crackle from the plane of intersection. Time stops within the plasma field.

Dab Tabmow says, "Young mutant, what is your name and where do you dwell?"

"My name is Mutant Boy. I live in the camps."

The view switches back to full speed and Dab Tabmow now holds Mutant Boy in a bear-hug. The crowd goes crazy and the Grand Mayor gives the thumbs-up. The scene fades to the victor's banquet.

Dab Tabmow gazes at the assembled fat, drunken slobs with grease dripping down their faces. The slobs throw half-eaten churdle shanks to fat dogs who are so stuffed they can barely be bothered to move.

Dab Tabmow squints his disapproval of the seedy affair. He shouts, "MULTI-VISION TORNADO ATTACK, LEVEL ONE!" as he grabs all four corners of the vast tablecloth and twists it onto his walking stick to form an enormous bindle carrying every kind of food imaginable. He blurs his way to the camps in search of Mutant Boy's dwelling.

"Only the worthy shall feast tonight, buddy!" shouts Dab Tabmow.

Mudhosh paused the video. "Did you get that Dluhosh? His name is Mutant Boy-1. He's a mutant from Planet One! He becomes Dab Tabmow's right-hands man. It's so radical that I can't even believe they allow it on television."

Michael and Gregory were getting frustrated that Miles kept running around chewing on and sniffing stuff where they were unable to see the video monitor.

"Hey, I have an idea," said Michael. "We need to train Miles to not get upset when our voices come out of him, and we need to get him to face the video monitor on command."

"That shouldn't be too hard, you know," said Gregory. "Quick, call him over, set him on your lap, and give him a treat. And then each time we speak, do it again. He'll associate our voices with treats. He'll stop freaking out, and we'll be able to watch TV."

Dluhosh called Miles over. Miles jumped into his lap and Dluhosh gave him a biscuit.

Michael said, "Can you give us something better? Like maybe some of that churdle bacon?"

They tried it again with bacon, and after a few repetitions Miles was trained and everyone was happy again. They put on another episode of *Dab Tabmow, ManCricket.*

Like a Swamp Master's slime, the old ways can slough off and return again when needed.
~ O'Buzznid-3

CRICKET LIAISONS

"Crickets?" asked the matronly Cricket Presidential Travelling Secretary upon meeting Buster and Zelda and their brothers and sisters. "I think the President was expecting young Bears…"

"Nope. We're Crickets, ma'am," said Buster.

"It's true that we are biological Crickets," said Zelda. "But we've been raised by Bears. It's very complicated."

Buster tried to hug the Presidential Travelling Secretary.

"Sonny, you do not want to get that close to me. I have not eaten today," she warned. "You do not speak like Crickets – and no one has chastised you for this?"

"No ma'am. Our Uncle Dee says that our Cricket accents make our Bear words sound adorable," said Buster.

"I guess it does… But you should avoid using so many contractions, and avoid initiating hugs with anyone but Bears, okay?"

The young Crickets nodded.

"Now, let me get this straight. The President chose you to be liaisons to his executive agencies, but did he say anything about limits on your powers? Your summer jobs are being created by presidential decree, and the way this is written makes you, in effect, a Presidential Commission."

"Ma'am, he said that we would submit reports to help him keep his government from spinning out of control while he was fishing," said Buster. "He wants ideas and pictures too! Uncle Dee says so."

"Fine, then let us begin processing you all for security clearances, and figure out what you would like to do for jobs."

She told them all to line up and stand at attention. She printed out the proper forms, grabbed a clipboard and pencil, and pointed at Buster.

"You first. But ALL of you listen, because I am only asking these questions one time. State your full name. State your primary aptitude – and I only want ONE. And apart from your primary aptitude, state your primary interest. I shall use this information to make your agency assignments as interesting for you as possible. Okay."

"My full name is O'Buzznid-3 Junior Buster-15."

"Wait! What?" said the Presidential Travelling Secretary as she absentmindedly bit her pencil in half.

"O'Buzznid-3 Junior Buster-15, ma'am."

"Hold on. I am not able to fit that on my form. You cannot have two numbers, young man. And did you say O'BUZZNID-3 JUNIOR?"

"Yes, ma'am. I'm sorry ma'am. He is my real father."

The matronly Cricket jumped three feet straight up into the air. "There is no need to feel sorry for me, sonny. For I knew your father, of course. At the inauguration of Rim Ram-1, we… we coordinated agendas. Sonny, you may be the most interesting thing that has happened to me since then. These Presidents, I just do not know…"

She laughed for the first time since witnessing a former First Lady almost drown in slime when a Swamp Master jubilee broke out during the ceremony to induct Swampy-12 into the Galactic Pool. She regained her composure and pointed at Buster.

"Ma'am, my primary aptitude is command, and my primary interest is playing the *Dab Tabmow, ManCricket* video game."

"The what?"

"The DTMC…? You don't know about the *Dab Tabmow, ManCricket* show?" asked Buster.

"No, sonny. Elaborate."

"Oh gosh, where to begin…? Okay, here, we'll sing the theme song. We all know it by heart. Ready everyone?"

All one-hundred and fourteen Crickets sang.

Dab Tabmow was a man
He was a big man
He was also half Cricket
And talked like a Bearman
And accurate as a Dnooblian was he!

From the eleven-framed sunglasses on top of ol' Dab
To the claw of his churdle-hide boo-oo-oots
He was the flippingest twistingest kickingest hero
That the Galactic Pool ever knew-ew-ew!*

The President's Travelling Secretary sat down on the floor. "And this is on television, you say?"

"Yes, ma'am. It's by Trukk-9. And my Uncle Dee is his best friend! That's why Dab Tabmow talks like a Bearman.

Just like us! And we got to be in one of his shows – speaking parts too. We got paid scale!" said Zelda.

"I see. Then by all means, LET'S get you assigned to your agencies right away." The Presidential Travelling Secretary experienced Cricket frisson as she pronounced a contraction for the very first time since leaving the old country.

Once she had them all entered into the system, the secretary said, "Alright, there are not enough agencies for you each to have your own, so you will double or triple-up, depending on the size of the agency. Buster and Zelda, as you two are seniors with command and leadership aptitudes, I am assigning you to the Discreet Service at the Presidential Palace on Planet One. This will be a challenging assignment, but I expect you to observe all aspects of the agents' work, and send written reports to me weekly. Do you think you can handle that?"

"Yes ma'am!" they both said.

"Good, please prepare to leave this evening. I will call ahead and get things arranged well before your arrival. OK! NEXT! Walloper and Crush, you are assigned to the Galactic Broadcasting Company – same thing, observe and recommend. Please step over here. NEXT! Huggington and Snuggs, you are going to the Department of Health. NEXT! Biff and Boff, you are going to the Bureau of Insectoid Affairs. NEXT…"

***

Buster and Zelda arrived at the Presidential Palace. All of the staff insectoids were expecting them. They sailed through security and were permitted to walk unescorted through the maze of hallways to the Discreet Service offices.

As they walked through the Presidential Wing, two humanoids came down the hall toward them.

"Hiya buddies!" said Buster as they passed.

The two humanoids – a pale fleshy one in a midnight-blue robe, and an old mean-looking bald one – gave each other surprised glances, but they otherwise ignored the two Crickets.

"Those folks must have a lot of important things on their minds," said Zelda as they were buzzed into the Discreet Service headquarters office.

"Hello. You are from the Presidential Liaison Commission, correct? We've been expecting you," said the nervous humanoid receptionist. "We trust that you will find everything to your liking. Please let us know if anything displeases."

"For starters, I think we all need a hug!" said Buster.

"By all means, sir." She hugged Buster and Zelda in a three-way. It was the first time she had ever touched an insectoid.

The receptionist took a moment to recover. "Um, if you would like to start work right away, I think we have a detail headed out for duty right now. They are supposed to escort the Vice President and the President's chief advisor over to the Galactic Assembly for a meeting."

"Yay!" said Zelda.

"Alright. Wait just a second, please," said the receptionist.

"A unit of four rank-and-file Discreet Service agents came stomping into the office. They were dressed in body armor and carried automatic disruption cannons.

"Okay, we're out of here," said the crew leader. "We're hauling Number Two and the Fat Man over to the GA."

"Good, these two will accompany you."

The crew leader looked down at Buster and Zelda. "What is it, take your Cricket to work day?"

"Did you not get the memo, Group Captain? Buster and Zelda are from the Presidential Liaison Commission. They are efficiency-of-command specialists who report directly to the President. They are granted full-access clearance. You are directed to be polite and candid, Group Captain. Be sure your men behave themselves."

The group captain regarded them. "Say, it looks like you two have built-in body armor, so let's go."

***

Buster and Zelda rode in the trailing escort limo with the group captain and a junior agent driver.

"Those two guys passed us in the corridor today. They must be pretty important," said Zelda.

"Important? You don't know who they are? Really? The grumpy one is Vice President Griffer-1. You two must come from very high up. I suppose when you report directly to the President, everyone else is just another politician," said the group captain. "So what do you want to know from us?"

"Oh, I don't know, Chief. How about telling us what you guys are into," said Buster. "You know, what do you like to do when you aren't working?"

"Huh? The President wants to know that?" asked the junior agent.

"No, but I do, buddy."

"Buddy? You remind me of Dab Tabmow the way you talk," said the junior agent.

"Yeah! You like Dab Tabmow?" asked Buster.

The group captain asked, "What's a Dab Tabmow?"

The junior agent explained. "It's a new TV show by Trukk-9. Dab Tabmow is a superhero that's half Cricket and he goes around helping the downtrodden and stuff. And he talks like a Bearman, like Buster and Zelda."

"That's because our uncle is a Bearman who is best friends with Trukk-9. We even got to be in an episode of Dab Tabmow this summer. It's the one with snarlbeasts in it, but it hasn't been on TV yet," said Zelda.

"Really!? Hey, you guys are pretty cool," said the junior agent. "I can't wait to see it. Wow, Dab Tabmow…"

"And he has a totally awesome video game too!" said Buster. "You guys ever play it?"

"Of course!" said the junior agent. "I love that game. There's nothing else like it. It's probably my favorite thing to do. Tell the President that."

Zelda said, "They say it helps build hand-eye coordination, so it probably helps you shoot real bad guys."

"Yeah, you agents don't play it at work? You should." Buster took out a note pad and wrote down this thought.

***

When they arrived back at the Presidential Palace, Zelda followed the Vice President into his office.

Griffer-1 was surprised to find a little companion staring at him over the edge of his desk. "Excuse me?" he said.

"Hi, buddy, how you doin'? You're the Vice President, huh?"

The Vice President, shocked, asked, "May I help you?"

"Maybe. My daddy was General O'Buzznid-3."

"Who?"

"General O'Buzznid-3 – your former Vice Presidential Cricket…?"

"Oh, oh yeah. Sure. He was a credit to his species. Um, how did you get in here?"

"I work here. I am a Presidential Liaison Commissioner."

"A what?"

"It's my summer job. I have to go back to school in the fall, but right now I'm supposed to write reports and draw pictures of my experience here. Is it okay if I sketch you?"

"No, not right now. Is there something else I can help you with?"

"You bet. I was wondering if my father left any personal files that I might be able to see."

"They burn that stuff after Crickets retire. There's an incinerator in the basement. You'll find some kind of technician if you go down there. It may be able to help if you aren't too late."

***

Zelda found her way to the basement. She hugged the Praying Mantis clerk, introduced herself, and made her request. The clerk seemed delighted to help.

"No, Zelda, we would never burn your father's records. They are a galactic treasure. I bet you would love to see them. Come with me."

The clerk led Zelda toward a door that was painted with INCINERATOR – DO NOT ENTER. They entered. "Do not worry, it is quite alright. The sign is a decoy."

They passed through a chamber that looked like an incinerator to Zelda, and continued through to an unmarked door. "Welcome to the New Great Library of the Insectoids."

"Gosh! How far back does it go?" asked Zelda.

"If you mean physically, the halls radiate out from here in a semicircle with a radius of over one mile. Many Ants dedicated their lives to building this gallery. And many more of us dedicate our lives to curating the document collections. Every item is duplicated both digitally and on paper. But if you mean how far back this goes in time, the primary collection began shortly after the Insectoidicide Wars. So it is essentially a continuation of the Great Library of ZZZZZZ-3, but we have salvaged many documents from old Planet One archives as well – so it goes back many hundreds of years, but in pieces. If the Planet One humanoids found out about this, they would surely make us destroy it – so not a word, you understand?"

"Yes, ma'am."

"Good. Now, everything is cross referenced by topic and persons to which the topic pertains. To locate your father's main records, go up this hall approximately one-half mile to the isle marked O dash two. You may also browse around if you like. When you are finished, return here and clock out."

"Can I make copies of things I want to share with my brothers and sisters."

"By all means, darling. There is a scanner at the end of each passage. Enjoy!"

Zelda looked up and saw the large A-1 that marked the A-1 isle. On the left corner she saw a drawer marked AARDVARK. She didn't know what that was, so she took a quick look. She pulled up a folder with a single ten-page document in it. The cover page read: *AARDVARK: Studies of the animal called 'aardvark' from the planet Bounty-2 for potential application as a weapon.*

Zelda flipped through the document. There were several photographs of the horrifying beast in its original habitat. The final page of the document read: *The animals are effective at tearing things apart and eating insectoids, but they appeared much larger in the original photographs. Any further investigation into weaponizing the aardvark should focus on genetic enhancement of its body size. End.*

"Yikes. I'm glad Bounty-2 is a lost planet!" said Zelda aloud. She was amused as her echo came back to her.

She walked to the next letter - the B-1 row. The first drawer was marked BAARP. Zelda couldn't resist having a look. Again, it was a thin file. It contained a single sheet of paper, which was stamped: *BAARP (Galactic Autotranslator Recalibration. See Griffer-1, O'Buzznid-3).* And the document itself said simply: *No records to be maintained.* And it was an original document signed by President Rim-Ram-1 himself in ink.

"Ha! Rim Ram-1!" said Zelda. Her exclamation was followed by HA HA HA HA HA RIM RIM RIM RIM RIM RAM RAM RAM RAM RAM ONE ONE ONE ONE ONE… echoing through the catacombs.

My Daddy mentioned this duty in his book, she thought, and turned to skip away to the O isle.

She waved at a couple of research librarians in the H isle, paused to contemplate a drawer marked JAMDOWN RECORDINGS (CLICK BEETLES) at the J-1 isle, and took a hard right turn at the O-2 isle.

She found the drawer marked O'BUZZNID-3, GENERAL, VICE-PRESIDENTIAL CRICKET. She pulled the drawer out and found files marked with the names of every vice president from Bouffer-1 up to Griffer-1. The files were of varied thickness and filled the length of the drawer. In addition to the folders, along the edge of the drawer she noticed a cardboard tube marked BAARP.

Zelda popped the plastic cap from one end of the tube. She turned the tube upside-down and shook out a rolled-up document. She unrolled the single sheet. It was a map. She could not read the lettering, but the cartography was clear.

I've found the map to the galactic autotranslator, she thought to herself.

"I found it Uncle Dee!" DEE DEE DEE DEE DEE…

Respect the truth; deceive the deceiver. Seriously, screw them if they cannot tell the truth.
~ O'Buzznid-3

PRESIDENTIAL DECREES

Her alarm triggered the auto-open sequence, and the Presidential Travelling Secretary bounded out of her stasis box. She looked around the hotel suite – still no sign of the President. The single plastic shrub in the room only made her miss her exotic plant collections even more.

She retrieved some documents from the printer basket. She smiled to herself when she saw the first set of weekly reports from the Presidential Liaison Commission. And buried under these reports was the first quarterly earnings statement from the recently expanded Galactic Broadcasting Company.

The top liaison report was from the senior crew assigned to the Discreet Service, Zelda and Buster. Their report read:

Gosh, this is so cool. The insectoids in the Presidential Palace are very nice to us. Everyone is totally into Dab Tabmow! Even most of the humanoids in the Discreet Service are into Dab Tabmow. We get to ride with the agents when they take the Vice President and the fat guy places. Sometimes the important guys give us funny looks, but the only humanoids who talk to us directly are the agents. They seem very bored. When they aren't giving rides to people, they write reports about giving rides to people.

If we could make some suggestions to help out this agency, we would recommend requiring the agents to play the Dab Tabmow, ManCricket *video game in place of writing boring reports. This activity would make them have better hand-eye coordination and would help them defeat bad guys better. And we think the incinerator should be equipped with higher resolution and larger format digital scanners. Buster and Zelda.*

Under the text is a drawing that depicts an assassination attempt on Griffer-1 and Gro Skoo. An agent is kicking the bad guy's gun out of his hand. A thought bubble containing a drawing of Dab Tabmow is shown coming from the agent.

The Presidential Travelling Secretary smiled and read the second report.

We report from the headquarters of the Bureau of Insectoid Affairs. Could we please get moved to someplace more interesting? The first thing we noticed was the lack of insectoids here. There are a few administrative Crickets with their Blister Beetle boss, but all of the managers are Planet One humanoids who seem mostly interested in finding out where a bunch of lost money went.

If we could make a suggestion it would be this: Bring in some more insectoids. The managers have very large offices that could easily accommodate one representative from each ZZZZZZ-3 insectoid species. They could be a lot of help to the managers, and would definitely liven things up around here. Biff and Boff.

Below this is a full-color drawing of a BIA official's office with extra desks in it. Behind the desks, which are bigger than the official's desk, are seated what appear to be an Ant, a Tiger Beetle, a Pleasing Fungus Beetle, a Mantis, a

Bee, and an imaginary Wasp with riveted copper mandibles and fire shooting from its maxillary palps.

She shook her head, smiled again, and read another report.

This is Walloper and Crush with our report from the Galactic Broadcasting Company. It has been very interesting here because it is so busy and frantic and we get to meet some people that we have seen on television. The managing executives tell us that ever since the President signed the decree to expand the number of GBC channels from five to five-hundred, there has been a huge burst of creativity and revenue. We have no recommendations at this time.

Below this is a crayon drawing of a young female humanoid wearing a swimsuit and high heels rolling around in a pile of money with what appears to be a television executive. Hunky, shirtless gardeners with leaf blowers maintain the perimeter of the money pile.

The Presidential Travelling Secretary hoped that the picture was just a scene from a silly TV show of some kind. But she skipped ahead to the GBC earnings report to look for clues. This report was much thicker than usual. Also, the report's glossy cover featured a color picture of Jimmy Fresneaux with a caption that said: J-FREZ AND THE PREZ! FISH ON! And there was an inset image of Dab Tabmow spinning into a tornado with a caption meant to convey his trademarked tummy thunder. The red GBC logo, which had always been the only decoration on a matte gray cover, was now partially covered by Jimmy's big bass. She turned to the earnings summary, went right to the bottom line, and gasped through all of her spiracles.

***

The Presidential Travelling Secretary completed her review of the liaison reports and took the liberty to prepare presidential decrees for several items that she thought were particularly good ideas.

She had one of the Discreet Service guys take her to the President's location – Jimmy's boat – for their weekly briefing.

"Can't it wait? Me and Jimmy are into some big ol' mossback sowbelly bass right now," said the President.

"It's okay Mister President," said Jimmy. "You might as well get this out of the way before the evening bite starts anyway."

"Yeah, yeah, okay. What do you have for me, Travelling Secretary?"

"Sir, firstly, I thought you would like to know what the latest earnings statement from the GBC says."

"Did they break even this quarter?" asked the President.

"Sir, after implementing your decree, they have…" She whispered into the President's ear.

"Huh!?" said the President. "How many zeroes is that?"

"Sir, it is approximately equal to the quarterly budget of the Galactic Pool Government."

"Who does all that money belong to?"

"They are the people's airwaves. So the money belongs to the people, sir."

"I am a man of the people," said the President. "Do I get to help them spend it?"

"As a matter of fact, Mister President, the implementing regulations of the decree you signed require the Office of The President to hold the people's revenue in trust. You are now responsible for issuing additional decrees, at your discretion, to finance projects to benefit the people."

"I like spending money, Travelling Secretary, but how long is this going to take? And isn't this something Griffer's supposed to handle? What do the people want anyway?" asked the President.

"Here are the reports developed by your Presidential Liaison Commission, sir. They have some very intriguing ideas about what the people want."

The President's face screwed up like he didn't know who she was talking about.

"This lesion thing sounds pretty serious," he said. "It's mine?"

"Yes, sir, they are – you remember the Bearman's teenagers, right? Anyway, sir, to save time, I have taken the liberty to prepare some draft presidential decrees for your signature, in case you should want to implement the recommendations. Some of these initiatives do not cost anything, others will likely pay for themselves in the long term, and the rest are covered by funds from the GBC trust, which is probably growing faster than it can be spent. Here is a pen, sir."

"Can't I just sign them and get it over with? The evening bite…"

"Sir, I should recommend that you at least look at some of the reports so that I can say you did, if anyone asks."

"Okay, give 'em to me, Travelling Secretary." The President licked the tip of the pen. He glanced at Buster and Zelda's report and said, "Some guy is shooting at Griffer and Gro Skoo. Look at their butts! Heh heh, how could you miss butts that big? I didn't hear about this happening, Travelling Secretary."

"I think it is just an illustration of how the new Discreet Service agent training initiative would work, sir."

"And that could have been me! Where do I sign?" The President re-licked the tip of his pen and signed.

"Now this one provides universal health care for the residents of Scablands-17. This is one of the main recommendations of the liaisons to the Department of Health."

The President looked at the picture.

The first frame depicts sick and injured dwarf humanoids who have two hands on one arm and a bony hook on the other. They are rolling around in the street with action lines around their mouths to indicate that they are coughing. The second frame shows the same Scablands-17 humanoids in clean hospital beds with big smiley faces.

"My goodness, I see. But why does it have to be universal? The Scabsters are part of the Galactic Pool, right? Could we save money by just giving them galactical health care instead?"

"Very good point sir. You can go ahead and sign the decree and I will make the necessary changes later. Now this next decree would allow insectoids to use contractions, sir."

The President signed it and said, "Of course, insectoids need contraptions just like everyone else. The right tool for the job, I always say."

"I'll have to agree with you on that one," she said with pride.

"Good. Are we almost done?"

"Just a couple more... Here's one for the Bullets-to-Bonbons Initiative. Thank you. The High Seas Marine Reserve Network on Flat Rock-13 – there you go. And augmentation of funds for your No Grub Left Bewildered program – right there."

The President signed them all and went back to casting.

The Travelling Secretary said, "I'll record these, sir, and with your permission, I'll be back next week with several more."

"Fish on! WOOOOOO!" said the President.

***

A week later, the Presidential Travelling Secretary returned with new reports and draft decrees.

"Fish on! YES! That's one-hundred casts in a row. Hot damn! Jimmy, you are a magician at finding the bass," said the President.

"We need a break anyway," said Stick.E from his hovering cloaked utility saucer. "I need to recondition these fish. Fin wear is becoming an issue and I need to resurface the insides of their mouths."

"Okay, Secretary, what do you have for me this week?" asked the President.

"Sir, the first report is from your Presidential Liaison Commissioners at the Bureau of Insectoid Affairs."

She showed the President the report's elaborate drawing.

It depicts a lifeless landscape with scattered dead insectoids, each with many tiny X's for eyes. Some sort of foaming goo covers everything.

"Yikes! Dang, what is this!?"

"Sir, I'll read you their report. It says: *We saw pictures of the Liberation of the Insectoids during a presentation at the BIA. It was a war from a very long time ago. It made us very sad. Dab Tabmow would not allow this. They told us that their planet was still poisoned and they couldn't live there anymore, not even the Cockroaches. They want to know why it was possible to give Chuffed-18 a whole new terraforming, but not ZZZZZZ-3. Also, they still haven't found the missing money yet.*"

Jimmy Fresneaux said, "Yeah, you guys did a pretty good job on terraforming this planet. It's got some decent bassin' spots, and once all my little clone fingerlings grow up, I think Chuffed-18 will be a destination bassin' resort for the whole galaxy. But, boy howdy, if you could start from scratch… Dang, I could create a true Hawg Heaven. Just think – there would be a topwater bite happening somewhere in the world every minute of every day!"

"Really? You could do that?" asked the President.

"I could design it, for sure. You guys can replicate lily pads and big ol' stumps, right? We could make lakes with lots of nice drop-offs at the perfect depth for Chompy Chunkbaits. We could have submerged islands with brush-piles on top. Oh, and I'd definitely have some big lazy rivers with deep dark holes where you could accidentally hook a great big catfish. It would be awesome!"

"Well, there you have it. Travelling Secretary, please write up a presidential decree that authorizes what Jimmy just said."

"Done, sir. Here you go – signature right there…"

He signed the decree and asked, "Um, Travelling Secretary, is this something we can afford? Remodeling a whole planet is expensive, right?"

"Yes, sir. But the funds from the Galactic Broadcasting Company can easily cover it. And in the long-run it will be good for the Galactic Pool economy, Mister President."

"Good. Authorize that too."

"You already did, sir," she said as she handed him the report from the Commerce Department.

The President scratched his head over the drawing.

The single frame shows what appears to be a Praying Mantis getting a paycheck from one humanoid and then turning around to give it to another humanoid who looks just like the first one.

"What does this mean?"

"Here's what the report says: *We think the insectoids should be allowed to shop at the same duplicators as everyone else. Shoot, the insectoid duplicators don't even sell Dab Tabmow games and everything is more expensive.*"

"Do the insectoid duplicators sell Jimmy Juice or Stanky Shads, ma'am?" asked Jimmy.

"Undoubtedly not. The Insectoid Company Store only sells basic supplies at inflated prices," replied the Travelling Secretary.

"That just ain't right! There should be equal access to the best soft plastic baits and energy drinks for all!" said the President.

"I agree!" said Jimmy.

"Sir, would you like to sign the decree then?"

The President snatches the decree and signs it with an extra-large signature. "That's so the Commerce Administrator can read it without his spectacles!"

"Thank you, sir. Now this one is from the liaison to the Discreet Service."

The President studies the drawing. It is a single panel that apparently depicts Griffer-1 with his hackles up, claws sprung, and little wavy anger lines coming out of his head.

"Heh heh, I recognize that look. What does it say?" asked the President.

"It reads: *This man gets very angry sometimes. Today we took him and the fat man to see some soldiers and he was rude to them. I think it was because they were insectoids. We have one recommendation this week. We think this mean old man should not be allowed to boss soldiers around like this just because they are insectoids.*"

"Those little Bears sure have the VP figured out. Heh heh, I hope you have a decree for this!"

"I do, sir."

"Really? I was just kidding. But what does it say?"

"It limits the Vice President's ability to boss the military around without your personal approval," said the Travelling Secretary.

"It's not like that already?"

"No, sir, right now the Vice President has the full power of the presidency. You granted him this authority via presidential decree."

"I did?"

"Yes, sir. This is why you have been able to go fishing for so long. Anyway, this decree would, therefore, just be a minor amendment to an existing decree."

"Yes, I'm definitely signing that! Griffer needs to learn to play nicely just like everyone else. His problem is that he never had any playmates as a child. Sad, really. So you got any more stuff for me?"

The Presidential Travelling Secretary was getting nervous about going too far with these decrees, so she just wanted to get out of there.

"No, sir. I'll be back next week sir."

Once the Presidential Travelling Secretary was gone, the President said, "Jimmy, I don't understand where the GBC is getting all that money. Are the airwaves really that valuable? Fish on!"

"Yes, sir. Fish on! For example, my production company buys advertising – millions of dollars' worth – every week. I'm selling enormous inventory via the airwaves."

"I don't – Fish on! – understand this 'advertising' thing you talk about. What is it?"

"You know, you've seen the ads for Slidewinder Reels and Jimmy Jams with the bikini models? Fish on!"

"Yeah… Fish on! I like those little programs," said the President.

"Those little programs are commercials, sir – advertising. You have five-hundred channels broadcasting to the whole galaxy. The ad revenues must be huge. Fish on! And now that insectoids can be customers, the ad value just went way up. But I tell you what, I can't sell anything on Scablands-17 for some reason."

"Yeah, that place is a shit-hole," said the President, holding his nose. "Fish on! Oh dang! I missed that one. Wait – there it is again… Fish on!"

"How many people live there? Fish on!"

"I don't know. A million, or a billion, or a trillion, or… Fish on! What comes after a trillion, Jimmy?"

"A trillion-and-one?"

"Yeah, something like that. There's a lot of them, but they're too poor to buy nice stuff. Fish on!"

"It seems like it would be a good investment to bring their wealth up, right? Fish on! If they had spending money, I'm sure I could move a lot of units of Jimmy Juice there. You know, you take the money from rich people like me who spend on advertising and give it to poor people to make them wealthy enough to buy more of my stuff."

"So, you mean, like – Fish on! – redistribute the wealth for the benefit of all?"

"That sounds kind of commie, Mister President. Fish on! But you could call it something like Market Stimulation Initiative and stick it in a presidential decree."

"Fish on!"

***

Back in the Presidential Palace, the newest Vice Presidential Cricket – Buzzy's replacement – was awoken automatically first thing on Monday morning. He got stretched out and went to check the mail. It was mostly another stack of presidential decrees from the Presidential Travelling Secretary. He reviewed them. He reviewed them again to be sure he wasn't imagining things. Then he had to take a moment to regain his composure before his weekly update with the Vice President.

"Good morning, sir. We have another set of presidential decrees."

"Not again... What does he want this time?" asked Vice President Griffer-1.

"The first one is for the GBC. Apparently Dnooblians are dangerous to work with in live dramatic acting, so to make up for the lack of Dnooblians in prime-time television, the President wants to decree that more cartoons starring Dnooblians be created."

"Are you kidding me? Are the decrees all like this again?"

"Let me see, sir. The next one would declare Chompy Chunkbaits to be the official chunkbait of the Galactic Pool."

"Look, I don't have time for the President's nonsense. How many more are there?"

The Vice Presidential Cricket showed the stack to the Vice President.

"Alright. You just go through them and set aside any that you think might cause a disaster. Then send the rest out to the appropriate agencies for implementation. And if any of the administrators make a stink, just tell them to do their best."

"Will do, sir."

***

The Presidential Travelling Secretary auto-awoke for her weekly reports from the Presidential Liaison Commission. They were in the printer basket as usual, but this time there was a cover sheet with a tarsus-written message that said: I LOVE the work that YOU do. Yours, VPC.

She noticed the curious capitalization. She imagined what the new Vice Presidential Cricket might look like –

like a young O'Buzznid-3 perhaps. Young like Buzzy was back in the days when… She didn't allow herself to finish the thought, but she did find herself hoping that she would live long enough for the new Vice Presidential Cricket's head to start itching.

She looked first at the report from Buster and Zelda.

We still don't like the very yelly man who we think is the Vice President. He gets angry too much. We think he is going to have a heart attack. We like his personal Cricket though because his Cricket is funny and he does a funny impression of Dab Tabmow. He joked that he wished he had a fire extinguisher full of calming agent to spray at the angry man. We think that is a good idea because it could save a life, so that is our weekly recommendation. We hope you like the drawing.

The drawing is in three panels. The first shows Griffer-1 with his fists up and lightning bolts coming from his face. The second panel shows the Vice Presidential Cricket spraying Griffer-1 with a fire extinguisher. And the third panel shows Griffer-1 back at his desk with a big Cheshire smile on his face.

***

"WOOOO. FIVE bass on one cast! Son, this is the best topwater bite ever! I just love this Mega-Mouth Poppin' Minnow," whooped the President.

"Yeah, yeah, it's really awesome, Mister President," said Jimmy, stifling a yawn.

"Hey Jimmy, I got a joke for you. Heh heh… Knock, knock!"

"Who's there?"

"Heh heh…"

"Heh heh, who?"

"Huh?"

This joke may have been interrupted when the Discreet Service delivered the Presidential Travelling Secretary for her weekly briefing, but no one could be sure.

"Aw, man, do we have to do this now?" said the President.

Jimmy said, "Mister President, you must be getting hungry after stroking all those toads. Here's your sandwich if you'd like it."

"Yeah, thanks, I'd love a sandwich. Okay… What do you have this week, Travelling Secretary?"

"Sir, I can keep it brief. I only have one report and two draft decrees."

"Gimme…" said the President as he bit his sandwich and pointed at the picture on the top of the papers.

She held the drawing up in front of him.

The President almost choked on his sandwich while laughing.

"Sir, the liaison commissioners are afraid that the Vice President is going to drop dead in a rage someday. They want you to provide the Vice Presidential Cricket with a first-aid calming agent spray device."

"That sounds like a pretty good idea, but wouldn't it maybe be better to let nature take its course? I mean, is it right to be interfering in the natural succession of life and stuff?" asked the President, taking another bite of sandwich.

"Speaking of succession, sir, if the Vice President were to die, his successor would be the Leader of the Galactic Assembly."

"Who's that then?"

"Who? Um, Mister President, you have met him on several occasions. He is the Fermamentian Viscount with the big noses and curly mustaches."

"Oh, Mister Smelly Jelly Belly! That guy? Really? Would he have to move into the Presidential Palace?"

“Sir, his name is Viscount Shelly Nelly-4, and yes, you would be in close proximity to him often.”

“Okay, give the Cricket a nozzle then. But really, Mister Smelly Jelly Belly? Is there something I can do about that?”

“Yes – you can decree a different successor.”

“Who would you suggest, Travelling Secretary? How about Jimmy here? Jimmy, you wanna be vice president someday, son?”

Jimmy was asleep.

“Sir, my opinion is that the Vice Presidential Cricket would make a natural successor in the event that the Vice President were killed or incapacitated. He already knows everything, he is odorless, and he won’t yell at you. He’ll treat you with the utmost respect, and you can always name a different vice president once everything is under control.”

“Replacing Griffer with a Cricket… Now THAT is funny. Can you write me up a draft decree, Travelling Secretary?”

“It’s right here, sir.”

Crickets did not evolve these leg spikes for roasting marshmallows.
~ O'Buzznid-3

BABIES EVERYWHERE

Dee was back on Chuffed-18 to propose something to Trukk-9. He found Trukk-9 at his estate. Trukk-9 was just getting ready to head over to Fleence's estate. Kyleence had called to tell him that Fleence's big moment was about to happen.

"Skip! I have a map to the galactic autotranslator! My niece Zelda found it in Buzzy's archives. Look!" said Dee.

Trukk-9 examined the map. "Yes, we must go here. We must make a film of you fulfilling your destiny."

"Right, but I'm not exactly sure how to interpret this map. All of the writing seems to be encrypted. Wouldn't you know it? The stupid autotranslator has instructions that can't be translated! But it looks like Buzzy was trying. He left some notes in the margins. Just numbers though. What do you think they mean?"

Trukk-9 took a look. "Could they be coded coordinates? Let me run them by Stick while we head over to see Fleence, and hopefully Jimmy." Trukk-9 called Stick.E on the utility saucer at the fishing show production and explained the pregnancy situation.

Stick.E replied to Trukk-9 by yelling, "What? My mother is dying!? Oh, no!"

"Um, no…" replied the confused Trukk-9.

"My poor poor mother, she's gone tangent… WAAA WAAA!" cried Stick.E.

The President was resting in Stick.E's saucer after recovering from a sudden allergic reaction that he'd had after eating a sandwich. He had overheard Stick-E's lamentations. "Young man, I heard what you said. I'm so sorry. I hope your mother recovers. Now just go ahead and put me back in Jimmy's boat, and go do what you have to do."

"Thanks Mister President!"

Stick.E set the President in the back seat of Jimmy's boat.

The President said, "Hey, everyone. I'm all better! Let's get back to bassin'!"

Jimmy and the production crew woke up.

The President continued. "The blue wavy fella in the saucer said his mom is dying. He has to leave. I hope that topwater bite is still going off. WOOOOO!"

Stick.E explained via the director's headset that Jimmy's baby was about to be born.

The President made a cast. He let the Mega-Mouth Poppin' Minnow sit until all the ripples had died away. Then he gave it a twitch. Nothing.

"Hey! What's wrong? Did the bite die?"

"We can't catch anything now, Mister President," said the director. "Um, ah… Yeah, it's a condition of our environmental permits that the plasmanoid fella has to be here as an observer. The fish won't bite if he isn't."

"The fish know this?" asked the President.

"Yes, sir. Informing the fish is also a condition of our permits."

"Preposterous!" said the President. He took a cast with one of his Chutney Chump worms, which had been slaying bass all month long. The worm sank to the bottom and the President bounced it over a sunken stump. Nothing. "Dang. I guess you're right."

The director yelled, "That's a wrap!"

The Discreet Service agents hustled the President into the waiting limo saucer.

Jimmy collapsed onto the floor of his bass boat. They had filmed over seven-hundred episodes.

The phone in Jimmy's pocket buzzed. It was the midwife.

***

Dluhosh, Mudhosh and Miles/Michael/Gregory had arrived on Chuffed-18 a few days before. They confined Mudhosh to the ship, however. Dluhosh and Miles were in Fleence and Jimmy's house with Kyleence, Dee, Trukk-9 and the midwife. The midwife had never been present at a birth before. She would become a very good midwife during the next few weeks, but right now Fleence was in advanced labor and the midwife was very interested in what the little dog had to say.

Michael, via Miles, said, "I saw a film of it in health class one time. You have to feed the mother ice chips and tell her to push."

"And there's something about dilation, but I have no idea what that means," added Gregory.

So Miles ran around yelling 'PUSH' and looking for bacon to fly his way. Dluhosh fed ice chips to Fleence ten at a time. And the midwife tried to work out what dilation was.

Jimmy burst through the door, still dressed in his bassin' gear. Miles yelled 'PUSH' one last time. The midwife shoved Jimmy into position and he participated successfully in the delivery of the first ever natural birth by a Bountyan clone. The little girl weighed in at eight pounds and four ounces, so they named her Lunker-18.

"Oh Jacques, I knew you'd make it in time…" said an exhausted Fleence.

Jimmy said, "That last sandwich with the bee venom almost did the trick, honey. But I'm afraid it was Stick.E's mother's medical emergency that shut us down. Stick had to go see her."

Just then Stick.E burst in through the front door. He had taken the finely-detailed form of a churdle calf so he wouldn't spook any little babies.

"Sorry folks – my mom is fine. I had to come up with something to get us out of there. I think the President is genuinely insane," said Stick.E.

"Kyleence! What's wrong? Is it time?" said Trukk-9, as he noticed his wife looking down at her belly.

"I detect that her water has broke," came out of Miles' mouth.

"This is all happening so fast!" said the midwife.

Dluhosh fed ice chips. Trukk-9 got into position. Miles yelled "PUSH" has he drank out of the toilet. The midwife's water broke too. So Jimmy got back into position. And before they knew it, there were four babies crying.

Once the babies had latched on and things had settled down a bit, Kyleence said, "Michael, Gregory? Um… Come Miles! Good boy! There's something I need to tell you."

Miles came running in.

"You know who these babies' daddies' are, right?" asked Kyleence.

Miles was looking at the suckling babies, so Michael and Gregory could also see them.

"No," they said.

"Look closely. Do you remember?"

It dawned on Gregory. "Uh, we…?"

Then Michael figured it out. "Whoa, man…"

"Yes, you are their biological fathers! Isn't it wonderful? Trukk-9 will raise them as their adoptive father, of course, and you are the fathers of many more to come – soon. But it's magical!"

"Wait, how many babies are we fathers to? Nom, nom, nom," they asked while following something across the floor and then eating it.

"That's not a simple question. We have combined your genes in various ways before implanting. There are many combinations of you two and Jimmy. We even hope to get some babies with blue eyes. For example, there are versions of your sperm that will produce female babies with chromosomes from all three of you. We are trying to get as much genetic diversity as possible from a small sample. Deleterious recessive genes have been repaired. Oh, and Jimmy is providing the entire natural reproductive process as often as he can to lucky applicants."

Dluhosh said, "I guess it seems like a good time to explain to the rest of you why we came here so quickly from Dnooblia. You see, Michael and Gregory died in a tragic accident. I was unaware of the plasma leak until it was too late to save them. Luckily I had downloaded their full memories shortly beforehand. I was able to upload compressed memories into Miles. And it is also possible to transfer their complete minds into an infant by using my PLUMBOB memory wiper unit. So we have asked

Kyleence if we could clone them new bodies. I have some samples to work with."

Kyleence looked at the babies and then at Trukk-9 and said, "We owe Michael and Gregory so much…"

Trukk-9 gazed down at his new adopted babies and put his hands on their heads. "I think it would be appropriate."

"Hold on," said either Michael or Gregory. "Are you suggesting that we be uploaded into their little baby brains right now?"

"The sooner the better," said Dluhosh. "The more memories and personality the babies develop, the more difficult it will be to completely integrate your minds with theirs."

"But the babies are their own little people already. Look at them. They already have their own memories of being born and breast feeding and stuff," said Michael.

"It would be basically the same with a laboratory clone," said Dluhosh. "If you want a body, you have to hijack a mind as well."

"What will it be like?" asked Gregory.

"I'm not entirely sure. I would be transferring your entire minds, so it won't be like being in Miles. You will have your motor memories, but it might take a while for your neural pathways to develop. There could be a lot of frustrating flopping around, but you should be easy to potty train. There's also a lot of hormonal development that needs to take place, of course. Really, all I can say is it will be weird. On the bright side, you'll be the smartest boys in kindergarten."

"I suppose we have no choice," said Michael. "Are you guys sure you'd want to go through with it?"

Kyleence said, "I'm going to try for another set of twins as soon as possible anyway. I think it would be valuable to have your knowledge handy. We are about to experience the biggest baby boom in the history of the Galactic Pool, and none of us have experience with raising little boys of our species. Your presence would be very helpful."

"There is one other consideration," said Dluhosh. "Your full minds on the computer will not remember anything beyond our arrival at Dnooblia. It will not be THEM deciding to have themselves put into a baby brain, right? You guys need to speak for them and you will need to explain it to the babies. Are you sure it is what they would want?"

"Yes, and I'm pretty sure I can speak for Gregory," said Gregory. "But I think you should erase the memories we have of, you know, the thingy…"

"Excuse me?" said Dluhosh.

"Can you erase the parts where, you know… They're going to be our future mother and sister… Ahem. Remember? The kind words and all that…"

"Oh, you mean the brief telepathic erotic episodes. The growling and such behavior – that makes sense. Sure, sure…" said Dluhosh. "Erotic episodes show up quite clearly in a memory scan, so yeah, we can probably locate and extract them easily enough."

"Shall we do this then?" asked Kyleence.

They called Mudhosh to grabber-beam them up to the ship. Dluhosh performed a scan of Gregory's stored memory. He sought the erotic peaks from Gregory's earlier encounters with Fleence and Kyleence. "Okay, on the graph we'll see a pronounced peak at any erotic episode."

A very fuzzy line came up on the screen.

"Wait, something's wrong. I must have the wrong setting…" Dluhosh scaled up the view. "No, it's accurate. Hmm, Gregory, there are hundreds of peaks. Look at this – at least one a day going back from the morning of the day you died. Something's wrong."

"Dluhosh, just go back to the time we met Fleence and Kyleence and wipe all the peaks up to now."

"But Gregory, according to this read-out, you should have died years ago. How is this possible?"

"It just is, alright?" said Gregory.

"Yeah, erase mine too. Just do it. Don't be asking a bunch of useless questions," said Michael.

Dluhosh completed the procedure and then Mudhosh grabber-beamed everyone back to the house.

***

Baby Michael and baby Gregory had difficulty forming words with their infantile muscle control, but the galactic autotranslator read their adult minds well enough that they could speak intelligibly right away. Baby Michael said, "What the hell?"

Baby Gregory said, "Where am I?"

Dluhosh said, "Okay Miles, one of you had better do the explaining."

Miles licked baby Gregory's face and said, "I am your father."

Baby Gregory said, "NOOOOOOOOOOOO!"

The voices coming from Miles explained the situation as best as they could while sniffing at an interesting spot on the carpet. The babies made the same protests about having to displace the original minds, but they did not want to be cut-and-pasted back to Dluhosh's hard drive. So Michael-18 and Gregory-18 began their new lives as citizens of Chuffed-18.

***

Jimmy was eager to get caught up on Earth news, so he invited Miles to go fishing.

"Now don't let Miles eat any worms, and keep him away from hooks. Just sit him in your back bassin' chair and tell him to stay. And if you catch a fish, don't let him bite it," said Miles.

"Don't worry, we won't catch anything. Stick.E isn't here, and all the bass in this lake are still peanuts and bank-runners. We only have the original five bass big enough to film with, and it's their day off. Anyway, what's been going on? Has anyone tried to figure out what happened to me?"

"Yeah, it was kind of a big deal, actually. They did one of those unsolved crime TV shows on your case. They arrested your neighbor for the murder, but he was released even though he said he took a shot at your ghost. A lot of people think you were abducted by aliens. Your neighbor talked about seeing you fly and things like that. And they found a big divot at the bottom of the lake with your truck and trailer still parked there. Some people claim the divot could only have been made by space aliens. Anyway, your case is just one on a long list of things that space aliens are being blamed for."

"So what else is on the space alien list?"

"The melting of Mount Rushmore is the big thing of course. Those Planet One assholes really sent that ship to Earth. We failed to stop them. Plus, that big voice guy with the meteors is all worried that his bogus study of Earth is contaminated by aliens. He's threatening to take Earth back to the Stone Age."

"Dang, I guess I'm glad I left."

"Dude, are you kidding! Glad you left? You are rich and famous and have more special ladies than a rock star."

"Sure, but it IS a lot of work. I hardly have time to eat. Just look at me. My cheeks are gone."

"You look pretty ripped. Lift up your shirt."

Jimmy showed Miles his abs and said, "It's a lot of exercise doing the reproductive therapy ALL the time. In fact I have to go to an appointment soon. So what else has been going on?"

"Dluhosh hung around Earth and was curing diseases and acting like some kind of vigilante superhero, and that's getting noticed too. You know how it is, every time some strangely mutilated corpses show up people blame space aliens. All the normal UFO stuff – typical hysteria."

"Yeah, but this time… never mind. So the big voice guy is bothered by this? He's threatening Earth?"

"Right. He's trying to take us up to the brink of making the scientific discovery that would give humans the technology to have been able to create his people. If he can get us to the final step before we are influenced by aliens, he'll prove that foot-size is the driver of universal creativity, or something like that. It's apparently a very big deal in his world. If his experiment gets ruined, then he has to start over again – with us back in the Stone Age, if we are lucky."

"Huh… So you don't happen to know who won the Global Bass Bass-Off last year, do you?"

"No, sorry."

"Because that's probably the one thing I regret most – that I'll never get a chance to fish in the Bass-Off."

"I think you can do better than that. You can have a GALACTIC Bass Bass-Off right here once these little bass grow up, right? You know – start a club, get some uniforms and trophies or whatever. Invite celebrity contestants and have a TV show about it. Some of your special ladies running around… It would probably be huge. You can even do it with the grabber beams and have it be a team sport – one boat and one flying saucer."

"That would be cool! Yeah, if Stick.E can be my partner, I could probably win. Plus, we could have chapters and regional tournaments on all the planets." Jimmy was already imagining different Galactic Bass logo designs.

"Wait. All the planets?" asked Miles.

"Yep, we have shipped out little bass fingerlings all over. And crawdads too."

"Oh no. I mean THIS planet is terraformed, so it's kind of like whatever – plant whatever you got. But do you think it's a good idea to unleash a bunch of largemouth bass on natural planets? Bass are bad-ass, right? They have large mouths, right? Won't they eat all the native species and stuff? Plus, they are from Earth, so, well, look out."

"Yep."

"You gotta stop them."

"Can't. It's by presidential decree. And I think it's way too late anyway. I'm sure by now the bass have already invaded."

Though he may seem a jerk, do not dismiss the lessons of the Bear.
~ O'Buzznid-3

THE DUMPING

After a month or so of easy mothering, Kyleence felt it was okay to give herself a break from Trukk-9. "Sugar, why don't you get back together with Dee and go do whatever it is that he was so excited about. The boys are fine. My girlfriends are always here with their babies, so I have plenty of support. You seem restless."

"Dee's back at his kitten ranch with his family. But maybe I'll call him. You're right though, *Dab Tabmow* is doing quite well in syndication, and I could use a new project. Maybe I'll drop a hint," said Trukk-9 as he dialed his phone.

"Trukk-9, take us with you! It's boring just laying here drooling," screeched little Gregory-18.

"Not until you can clean yourselves. This mission will be too hazardous for babies anyway."

Trukk-9 dialed his phone.

Dee answered. "Hugs to you. This is Dee."

"Dee! Let's go!" was all Trukk-9 said.

Kyleence said, "That was easy, pumpkin. You fellows already have it planned, don't you?"

"Yes, yes… I'm all fueled up, so I'm off to meet Stick.E. We will rendezvous with Dee at Free-15, and then catch a wormhole to Planet One."

"Hey man, don't forget to collect us any cool rocks you can find!" shrieked Michael-18.

***

The Cruiser Duke Sukk-9 was back in action, and the friends were filmmakers again.

"Alright guys, I was only able to guess at a few things based on this map and Buzzy's numbers," said Stick.E. "Again, we are only assuming that this thing is on Planet One, but Buzzy's coordinates are close to the tallest mountain on the equator."

"What exactly do we expect to find?" asked Trukk-9.

"It will in all likelihood be protected by a force field. So that raises an important question. Dee, will you be satisfied with dumping on a force field?"

"No way, buddy. Direct hit or nothing."

"We risk damaging the device though, right?" asked Trukk-9.

"I'd be very surprised if that were the case," said Stick. "A device this critical will have multiple redundant fail-safes. Force fields lose power all the time, so I'm sure the device is sealed up tight. Dee, your destiny doesn't require that you violate O-rings, does it?"

"No, Stick, I am the exact reason why they put those O-rings there."

"Alright, hopefully we find it, and hopefully I can deactivate the force field."

"Cut!" yelled Trukk-9. "Nice job guys. Let's do it again with the camera on Dee.

Dee and Trukk-9 moved the camera and lighting gear, then they took their places. Trukk-9 said, "Okay… rolling… and ACTION!"

"Alright guys, I was only able to guess at a few things based on this map and Buzzy's numbers…"

***

They were lucky. The device was on the top of the mountain. Actually, the device was perched on top of a five-hundred-foot tower on the peak of a tall mountain deep in a remote range.

Trukk-9 looked at the camera and said, "We have found the galactic autotranslator. It rests upon a needle upon a needle at the exact midline of the equator. This device is a transmitter, but for years it has been drawing my old friend Dee like some sort of hellish satellite receiver."

Dee moved the camera to include Stick in the background.

"My master technician, Stick.E-5, is working feverishly to decode the force field over-ride sequence. How is it going, Stick?"

"Piece of cake, guys. First try. The password was 'Rim Ram-1'! Those clowns are so predictable."

"Alright! I've been eating fistfuls of nuts and berries mixed with churdle lard all day. I think I'm ready. Let's hover over that sucker and I'll let 'er rip!"

"No no no. It can't be that easy. We must add stylizations, my friend. You must suffer, for this to be a truly epic quest – a destiny worthy of television," said Trukk-9.

Dee shot a glance at Stick, hoping for some support.

"He has a point, Dee. This is going to be a very short film otherwise."

Trukk-9 continued. "Dee, I propose that we drop you at the base of the mountain. You will climb the highest tower on the highest peak in the highest mountain range. This will symbolize that you do this for the highest purpose upon the highest purpose upon the highest purpose. Only then will the audience appreciate the real truth of the matter."

"You know, Skip, I've never fully understood your whole fake-it-to-make-it-truer philosophy of filmmaking. Look, what if we do this on a fly-by? I might miss a few times. I might miss a bunch of times. I'd have to eat pounds and pounds of nuts and berries. I'd suffer intestinal distress for sure, Skip. I'll roll around on the carpet and everything."

"Grab yourself some nuts and berries, my friend. We are dropping you on that talus slope at the base of the mountain. We will monitor you, but we won't intervene unless it's life-or-death. Oh, and pick up a couple of pretty rocks for my boys while you're at it," said Trukk-9.

Stick said, "Sorry Dee, he's right."

"Hey, wait a sec! How many times have I saved your life, Skip? If I hadn't picked you up on Dnooblia, you would have died of wasp stings and dehydration. And if I hadn't told Stick to grab you from that Swamp Master swimming hole, that swarm of baby eels would have swam right up your a-"

Stick grabbed Dee in his grabber beam and set him gently on the talus slope. Then he dropped him a supply of nuts and berries.

Dee ignored the nuts and berries and started right up the steep slope of loose rock. He gained one step for every three he took, but he trudged and cursed at the top of his lungs while shaking his fist at where he thought the cloaked Cruiser Duke Sukk-9 hovered.

"That's a good establishing shot, Stick. But it would be a much more truthful quest if it were snowing."

"No problem, Trukk-9."

And it snowed.

Still, Dee kept on trudging.

"Can you do hail?"

"Sure, how big do you want?"

"Make the hail the size of nuts and berries to symbolize the connection between the quest, the quest seeker, and the internal struggle."

Stick punched some buttons on the duplicator and shot hail from his custom array of grabber beams.

"Right. Look at him though. He just keeps on trudging."

"What should we do once he gets into that forest?" asked Trukk-9.

"I could knock some trees down in his path."

"Perfect. Try not to hit him."

Dee continued to trudge as he climbed over freshly fallen trees.

"Well, he travels like a Bear alright," said Trukk-9.

They lost direct sight of him as he trudged through a dense stand of saplings. All they could see was the even pace of disturbance evident in jiggling trees.

Dee emerged into a clearing and Trukk-9 said, "He's deliberately trying to ruin the shot! Why doesn't he fall down and eat some bugs, for crying out loud? At this rate he'll be to the tower by noon. He's gaining two-thousand feet per hour and all he does is trudge and shake his fist at us. And 'trudge' is the only useful word to describe this trek so far. He needs to scramble, and stumble, and scuffle. Even scooting would be more interesting than all this trudging."

They tried blasting Dee with high-decibel Planet One easy jazz. They tried piping the smell of a Fermamentian high school locker room at him. They bombed him with water balloons. They spray-painted him pink. Still he trudged.

Trukk-9 said, "If we coat the tower in churdle lard, would you be able to catch him if he slips and falls?"

"Sure, no problem, Trukk-9 – if he's high up enough I'll be able to snag him. So maybe I should just coat the top half of the tower…?"

"Packing peanuts!" said Trukk-9.

"Packing peanuts?" replied Stick.

"Yes. You know – the little squidgy things that go in boxes for shipping stuff."

"I know what they are, but what am I supposed to do with them? That's kind of arbitrary, don't you think?"

"You have a better idea? Don't worry, the packing peanuts will come to symbolize something. Now, can you build a mountain of them around the base of the tower? He'll have to fight his way up through the center of a two-hundred-foot mountain of packing peanuts just like a wild plug of lava ascending to its eruption! And the peanuts might cushion his fall if you miss with the grabber beam."

"A whole mountain? I'll have to crank all three duplicators up to ten and combine all primary grabber beams into a giant chute, but yeah… And I'll load them up with static electricity."

"Make it be," said Trukk-9.

Dee reached the base of the packing peanut mountain and trudged right into it without pausing – as if it weren't even there. He trudged through packing peanut hell, over jagged rocks, as static discharges zinged his extremities, until he ran face-first into the base of the tower. And up it he climbed.

Dee erupted from the peak of packing peanuts and right into the tower's churdle lard zone. He just kept right on climbing – vertical trudging, if you will – packing peanuts stuck to his pink fur.

"What a reveal! It looked more like a rocket shooting up through a great cumulus cloud than a wild lava plug erupting out of a volcano. But it's good symbolism for something! Okay, now we'll fly a full three-sixty around him as he struggles. Yes. It's beautiful. It's the purest kind of fiction. It is truth. Now we will know what this destiny really felt like to Dee. We understand. Yes, I know the perfect Dnooblian aria to play over this. I like my friend Dee very much. But what I don't understand," said Trukk-9, "is how he's going to get his rear end ABOVE the transmitter."

Dee made it to the top of the tower's latticework. Pink and peanutty and slick from churdle lard, he calmly got his grip on the opposite crossbeam and pulled himself into a handstand. When he was situated upside down with his knees locked around the tower's uprights and his cheeks spread, he let go with one hand and made a rude gesture at the spot where he thought Trukk-9's ship was. Then he grunted and hit his target like a marksman.

When they got him back on the ship, Dee placed two very pretty agates on Trukk-9's console and said, "Screw you guys."

The worst part of stasis is not knowing which nut-case will be in charge when you wake up.
~ O'Buzznid-3

MESSING WITH MOTHER ROOST

The two PLUMBOB verification agents sent by Gro Skoo to dig up bad stuff arrived at Mother Roost. The on-duty Cricket released his partner from stasis. They had done this kind of work together many times before, and they were good at it.

The first Cricket pulled up their official PLUMBOB checklist and searched for a computer network to help guide them to a population center. "They do not have much of a computer system. It looks like we are on our own for directions. I will try to scan for something. What low hanging checklist fruit would you prefer for breakfast today?"

"I think 'spontaneous road rage' would be delicious, me beauty! I wonder why the original PLUMBOB team did not find any of that?" replied the second Cricket.

The Crickets located a population center along an otherwise uninhabited coastline. They hovered over a busy intersection in their cloaked ship and waited to see if anything happened. After an hour of seeing nothing but well organized and courteous hovercraft, bicycle and pedestrian flow, the first Cricket said, "It looks like you had better jump-start the grabber beams and see if you can stir things up a bit."

"Will do. There, see that purple hovercraft second in line at the light? I am going to nudge it into the rear-end of the one in front. Got the camera ready?"

"We are good to go."

The second Cricket nudged the hovercrafts together. The two drivers waited for the light to change and then pulled over together at the side of the road. The Crickets pumped egocite around the drivers to activate the galactic autotranslator.

The 'at-fault' driver jumped out first and examined the damage. The other driver walked up and said, "Are you okay, partner?"

"Yeah, pal, I'm fine, but it looks like I dinged your bumper a little. Sorry about that. I'm not sure what happened – must have popped the clutch. My bad."

"It's no sweat. I think you actually nudged it closer to where it's supposed to be."

The two large shaggy birds shook wings and went on about their business.

The first Cricket said, "Too bad we do not have the good-stuff on the checklist. 'Spontaneous amicable resolution of automotive damages' is a rare item."

"But boring! I need to try a little harder. This time I will attempt to rack up a multi-hovercraft combination. Chalk please!"

The light changed, and as the hovercrafts entered the intersection, the second Cricket hit one of the stopped vehicles with the grabber beam like a cue ball, sending it into the cross traffic.

Overlapping hovercrafts formed a tight scrum in the center of the intersection. Steam hissed from a few, and one small fire had to be extinguished. Feathers were ruffled, beaks were bent, and hovercrafts were totaled. But after the momentary chaos, everyone stopped to help and tend to the various minor injuries.

"Dang,' said the first Cricket. "They are not even trying to assign blame. What is this – some kind of pathological mellowness that they are causing us to suffer?"

"I have another idea. You see that outdoor café over there?"

They flew to the café and tripped a waiter carrying a tray of muffins and hot drinks. The food and steaming liquids spilled all over a group of feathered businesswomen who had been enjoying a long lunch.

"They are laughing!" said the first Cricket. "What is wrong with these people?"

"No wonder bad stuff is at such a premium here," said the other Cricket.

"Hey, here comes one carrying a load of groceries. You ready?"

A young cock strutting down the road lurched into the path of an elderly hen. Her grocery bags crashed to the ground sending suet and sunflower seeds into the path of a bicyclist. The big bird on the bike took a header, and suffered a slight tear to his comb when his head scuffed the pavement.

The young cock begged their forgiveness and helped clean up the mess. Then he walked the elderly hen home to make sure she wasn't hurt. The only thing she cared to say about the accident was, "It's okay, young man. These things happen. Here, have a muffin."

"Incredible," said the second Cricket.

"This could just be a cultural phenomenon. There may be other places where the people are mean and nasty. Shall we try a different continent, old bean?"

"You are always so optimistic! And your optimism is contagious. Yes, I think we will find some extra itchy types over… let us see… that way!"

The Crickets shot across the ocean and turned left when they hit land. It was early morning there, and they followed the shoreline for hundreds of miles without seeing a sign of civilization. Then they rounded a cape with a large seastack on its point, and were shocked by what came into view beyond the rock.

A battleship.

"Hey! That is the Battleship Aedeagus! The one that was lost with Captain O'Spotnid-3 aboard…" said the first Cricket.

"I did not know about that," said the second Cricket.

"All presumed lost were insectoids, so it did not make the news channel. I worked on a mission with the Dung Beetle navigator once. He was actually a really nice guy between meals."

"How long ago was it lost?"

"Half a year, about… Hey, smoke!"

The huge battleship looked to have been pushed ashore by large storm waves. It sat at an angle with the starboard side sticking up into the trees, a swath of which it had apparently knocked over in making room for itself. A trail led from the ship's main hatch and disappeared into the forest behind the dunes. Another trail led through the beach grass on the upper dunes down to where the smoke came from. Just above the beach-wrack there were a couple of the large avianoids at a driftwood fire preparing breakfast.

"Uh, oh. Are those horrible birds eating what I think they…" began the first Cricket.

But they saw Captain O'Spotnid-3 disembark the ship with the Ant doctor. They both jogged down the trail carrying little flat boats.

"What do we do now?" asked the second Cricket.

"Good question. I do not see any immediate emergency, so I think we should just remain cloaked and observe. Hopefully something terrible happens."

***

On the ground, breakfast was almost ready. The insectoid crew had become accustomed to eating natural food cooked by the Roostians over a beach fire or in their sand ovens. And the Roostians had been having fun trying the alien recipes from the ship's duplicator. The high-oil seafood cuisines of Dnooblians and Flat Rockians were especially popular, and a few of the guys had developed an appreciation of Snake Ape savory country pies and the unleavened breads of Rumbly-11.

One of the Roostians grabbed a shovel and dug an iron cube from the sand and coals at the edge of the fire. He opened the small vault and removed two steaming muffins. He handed them to Captain Spotty and Doctor Exoskeleton.

"Thank you, gentlemen. How does it look out there this morning?" asked Captain Spotty.

"Well, Cap'n, we have a nice right break developing out on the point. It should start to get hollow once the tide lets it feel the reef a little more. Some of the set waves have a nice peel already. As it warms up, we should get a light offshore breeze. It's going to be another epic day, space groms! Have another muffin! This one has extra sugar, Doc," said Dayv.

The Dung Beetle came out of the woods. "Thanks for leaving me breakfast, gents. It is starting to shape up pretty decent out there."

"It's already as good as an old body surfer like you needs! What's keeping you?" asked Dayv.

"Banzai!" yelled the Dung Beetle as he took off and flew out to be first in the line-up. He had become quite a good swimmer, and could shred just as easily with or without a board.

The Bee engineer flew out of the ship and put his mug of honey on a hot rock by the fire. "I am still sore from yesterday. I am not even looking at the surf until after I have had my honey. Morning."

A couple more surfers came jogging down from Dayv's cabin. "Mornin' cats," one of them chirped. They pulled their muffins out of the vault and sat up close to the fire.

"Who's that on dawn patrol?" one of them asked.

Everyone looked up to see the Dung Beetle drop in. He made a clean bottom turn and pulled a floater on his back across the top of a pretty decent barrel.

"Oh, it's Dunger! Right on. Look at him go," said the other surfer.

***

Up on the cloaked ship, the first Cricket said, "This is officially weird. Are you getting this on video? This must be the 'communing with energy' checklist item that the first PLUMBOB crew got."

"Yes. But you know, I have read some shipwreck stories before. They seldom end up as happy affairs. Too much cannibalism for my taste. Normally the Dung Beetles are the first to starve, but my old colleague there looks fat and happy. Actually, it looks like he is having a lot of fun…" said the second Cricket.

"You sound tempted… You do realize, of course, that intentional contact with a candidate planet's inhabitants for non-checklist reasons is a class one felony? You also know what happens to Crickets in prison, right?" said the first Cricket.

"Yes, but, these people are already in a cozy little relationship with the crew of a battleship and a Captain of the Fleet," said the second Cricket.

"I am listening," said the first Cricket.

"I think it is either already too late and this place is going to be a default member of the Galactic Pool, or, if not, two more little PLUMBOB Crickets are not going to change anything anyway," said the second Cricket. "Plus, battleships do not carry memory wipers, so they are going to need ours to erase their tracks."

They turned up the outside audio receiver and sat in silence watching the morning unfold.

Down below they saw the rest of the crew, except the Moth technicians, paddle out into the surf. Dayv took his longboard out. One of the surfers went out on a stand-up paddleboard. Two surfers, including the guy with the new legs, kicked out on boogie boards wearing rubber webs between their talons. The Click Beetle joined the Dung Beetle in body surfing. The Moth technicians could be seen in the ship's viewing dome manning the egocite delivery tube and scanning for sea beasts. The Moths' fun-time would come in the evening around the bonfire.

Dayv worked to get the longest rides possible while hanging six off the nose of his board. Every minute in this condition felt to him like it added a day to his life.

After having added a full week to his life, Dayv invited Captain Spotty onto his longboard. “Okay, Cap’n, how many toes do you have?”

“Four claws count?” he replied.

“Hang four, daddy-o!” said Dayv. “I’ll paddle us into one of the outside rollers, and you stand up when you can. Hang your toes off the nose. That’s all there is to it!”

They paddled into a swell on the outside while all the other surfers and the two cloaked Crickets watched. Captain Spotty was up well before the wave started to break. Once he was securely hanging four, Dayv slid up to the middle of the board and said, “Hang on Cap’n, let’s try something.”

From behind, Dayv grabbed Captain Spotty by the edges of his upper abdomen and hoisted him up to stand on the top of his head. When the wave crested, Dayv was careful not to bury Captain Spotty in the pitching lip, and they added an easy day-and-a-half to their lives.

***

“Should we radio the Moths?” asked the first Cricket.

“Yes, I believe that it would be the proper protocol. I see little other choice.” The second Cricket punched the transmit button. “Ahoy Battleship Aedeagus, this is O’Hecknid-3 and O’Jecknid-3 aboard a PLUMBOB verification vessel presently hovering cloaked above your location. We are surprised to find you here. We are offering our assistance. How would you like us to proceed?”

After a moment, a voice came over the radio. “PLUMBOB ship, this is the Battleship Aedeagus, we do not require assistance at this time. Perhaps you would like to land on the beach and speak to Captain Spotty when he is done with his morning session. Over.”

"Moth technician, did you say that you DO NOT require assistance? You appear to be shipwrecked."

"Yes, we have lost power to the engines, but this is not a problem you can fix. Therefore, this ship is not going anywhere. It is the duty of the captain and crew to guard the ship from the local people."

"Who told you that?" asked the first Cricket.

"Captain Spotty," replied the Moth.

"Protocol dictates that we remove the locals, erase their memories, and sink your ship in the ocean until a salvage vessel can remove it," explained the first Cricket.

"Oh," replied the Moth.

"On the other hand, our sudden appearance would not change anything, would it?" asked the first Cricket. "How many locals know about you anyway?"

"Just these guys. And no, this location is isolated and there is no air or maritime traffic to see you. Why do you not just keep your vessel cloaked and come join us? We are getting ready for a bonfire barbeque," said the Moth. "And my partner and I will perform a traditional Moth dance once the fire gets going good. Oh, and you should get tuned up to rub some wings at the jamdown."

"I do not see that we have another option," said the first Cricket. He glanced at the second Cricket, who was already glancing back at him.

***

Doctor Exoskeleton and the Click Beetle formed an impromptu mandible and chest spike one-drop rhythm section. The Moths' bass wing-vibrations provided a solid bottom for the backbeat. Captain Spotty, the Bee engineer and the two new Crickets rubbed in different timbres to form a tight wing section. 'Dunger' sang a tune that he'd learned as a youth on the hard streets of a Planet One insectoid camp. Dayv picked his banjo, 'Blood' was on bongos, and the rest of the cats did their characteristic head bobbing flappy shuffle with the occasional high jump and syncopated honks at the edge of the fire's glow. Everyone joined in on the choruses.

We live in downpression, and it is a crime
We work for a dollar and they pay us a dime
We will not laugh upon their crying time
'Cause I am as free as a bird now

Free doot doot free
He is free from the herd now
No need to be spurred now
He drives a fast turd now

I look upon them and I say
Can you learn to be good today?
We will not ask you to pay
To be free as a bird now

Free doot doot free
They are free to be heard now
It is not so absurd now
To be second or third now

Big Planet One man, open your eyes
And come try my boots on for size
Then you shall get your prize
You are free as a bird now

Free doot doot free
Divisions are blurred now
It can be inferred now
I give you my word now
One flock of birds now

Doot honk-honk doot honk doot.

Each player took a solo. The Moths flew a do-si-do around the flames. The Bee shook his abdomen hard. And even Captain Spotty cut the sand with a jig from the old country.

A Cricket in a stasis box is able to fly as cargo. It is a great way to see the galaxy and you do not get hassled about time-shares.
~ O'Buzznid-3

WINDMILLS AND SNARLBEASTS

Somewhere out in the galaxy, about midway between Chuffed-18 and Mother Roost, Dluhosh searched for the next wormhole. Mudhosh searched for a particular episode of *Dab Tabmow, ManCricket.* And Miles/Michael/Gregory searched for a Dnooblian tennis ball that they'd almost chewed in half, and would finish if they could only find it.

"Dluhosh, can we just call Miles/Michael/Gregory by one name? It gets me all confused. Why not just call them Miles? Everyone knows what we mean," said Mudhosh.

Michael called out from under Dluhosh's bed, "That's fine with me! You, Gregory?"

"Yeah, you know, no big deal. We know who you mean," replied Gregory.

"There's our next wormhole," said Dluhosh. "ULBTX-123 has a lot of work to do if he's going to scrub out all of these. I hope he was exaggerating about space collapsing because this region reminds me of an old wooden sea pier riddled with shipworms. We're making good time though."

"Okay guys, I have it cued up. The Dab Tabmow show with Dee's teenagers in it!" said Mudhosh.

"This again?" asked Miles. "Aren't there some more of your videos from Mother Roost we haven't seen, Dluhosh?"

"NO! It's my turn to choose," said Mudhosh.

"Yes, but it IS Mudhosh's turn. We'll watch them after."

"Oh alright. Can you call us over then so we can see?" asked Miles.

"Here boy! Come Miles! Good boy! You just sit on my lap here fella. Good boy," said Dluhosh. He gave Miles a piece of churdle bacon, and Miles lay down in the curl of Dluhosh's hunting tentacles.

"This is the snarlbeast one right? Okay, so all I'm saying is that it's lame the way Dab Tabmow talks like some kind of sage to Mutant Boy, but like a back-slapping Bearman to everyone else," said Miles.

"Well you don't know anything, mister. Dab Tabmow is about ALL species, not just your humanoidcentric one," said Mudhosh.

"Look, man, we've seen A LOT of TV. You had, what, four or five state-owned channels until last year? Man, we're from EARTH – we've seen it ALL. This whole Dab Tabmow show can be boiled down to a one-word trope," said Miles. "Boring."

"Oh, you guys have no sense of aesthetics. Plus you keep falling asleep. You don't even understand…" said Mudhosh, hitting play.

The show opens in classic Trukk-9 fashion. The view is of a mysterious landscape, seen as if through a sheet of waving cheesecloth. It appears to be a valley as pondered from a mountaintop or the edge of a high cliff. The valley is dominated by windmills. The windmills power the giant pistons that hang within frames the size of lighthouses. These mysterious structures stretch as far as the eye can see. The windmills turn, and the pistons bounce as if trying to hammer something stubborn into the ground. The shot lingers and lingers and lingers. The pistons do not seem to make any progress. They just pound and pound.

Trukk-9's voice-over narrates. "Hundreds of them turn, though there is no wind to speak of… So each piston is manually operated by a pair of Crickets… What do these pistons do? What are they for?"

The camera pulls back to reveal Dab Tabmow and his sidekick, Mutant Boy, contemplating the scene below.

"This seems to be something of significance, Master. Have you a postulation upon this remarkable vista?"

"No," replies Dab Tabmow.

There is a pause.

"That's all? Just 'no'?"

"Shhhh, Mutant Boy. A pattern emerges… Listen."

"Turn up the subwoofer, Dluhosh!" said Mudhosh.

THUMP THUMP THUMPA THUMP THUMPA THUMPA THUMP THUMPA… and on it goes.

"Is it not just a bunch of random thumps, Master? Some of the pistons pound faster than the others, some of them stop and go at intervals, others are speeding up and slowing down. It's just a bunch of noise, right?" Mutant Boy puts two fingers and a toe into his ears.

"No."

"Just 'no' again? How am I supposed to learn anything? You fight so little and speak so infrequently anymore. You just answer all of my questions with either 'no' or some crazy random bunch of …"

Dab Tabmow raises his hand. Mutant Boy shuts up.

"Listen. They come together and then go their separate ways. Like the matings of churdles."

"Who does?"

Mudhosh paused it. "Gosh, Mutant Boy is so dumb sometimes. Dab Tabmow is always right, and Mutant Boy always learns a valuable lesson. Why doesn't he just listen and do smart stuff?"

Miles said, "See? Mutant Boy's dialog only serves to allow Dab Tabmow to be the quiet strong one. We already know that everything he says is the opposite of what Dab Tab-" Miles fell asleep again in the middle of the sentence, but this time Dluhosh didn't wake him.

Mudhosh hit play again.

Dab Tabmow says, "In ten seconds, one thump."

"What?" asks Mutant Boy.

The thumps coalesce into one giant THUMP.

"Wow, Dab Tabmow! How did you know?"

"Your ears are close to your brain for a reason, Mutant Boy."

"There you go again," says Mutant Boy as he tries to measure the distances between his ears and the center of his head.

Mudhosh said, "See that's Dab Tabmow's Dnooblian side coming through!"

"Shhhh, you'll wake them," said Dluhosh as he continued to softly stroke Miles' head.

The scene cuts to a front view of Dab Tabmow and Mutant Boy walking down a muddy path through thick vegetation. Dab Tabmow crouches to examine some spoor.

"Crickets," he says.

"HA! That's no Cricket poo, Dab Tabmow! That's snarlbeast poo."

Dab Tabmow thrusts the spoor in front of Mutant Boy's eye.

"OH! They ATE Crickets! I get it! Oh, wait, that's bad, huh?"

They take a few steps and see large clawed footprints in the mud. The mood of the background music is dark throat-singing and a solo Dnooblian cello. The music blends with the sound of the pistons. The two heroes walk on with heroes' purpose.

Mudhosh paused it. "Whoa, that was awesome. That scene! What a scene. Dluhosh, do you think when we go back to Chuffed-18 again that maybe I could meet Trukk-9 this time? Please. You said he smells good. I won't mess up. I just want to show him my paintings. I have some good ideas for him."

"We'll see," said Dluhosh.

Mudhosh hit play.

"HALT! Who goes there?!" yells an unseen person.

Mutant Boy jerks into his fighting stance. Dab Tabmow merely opens all of his eyes.

THUNK! A spear hits a tree behind Dab Tabmow, missing his bulbous head by just an inch. Mutant Boy spins his arms and legs into a single buzz saw. Dab Tabmow raises his hand and Mutant Boy stops.

"Cricket! We mean you no harm," says Dab Tabmow. Then he switches into Bearman mode. "Look buddy, we are just passing through looking for hard work and an honest wage. We see you've been having trouble with snarlbeasts. Those suckers need to learn a lesson. And I think we can teach them one."

A Cricket dressed in rags steps cautiously onto the trail in front of them. He cocks his head as he regards the two unusual strangers before him. Then a young female Cricket jumps onto the trail behind them.

Mutant Boy speaks. "Hey, take it easy there. This is Dab Tabmow. He is the best, I mean BEST, fighter in the land. He even defeated me! So just you watch out!"

"Hush," says the front Cricket, played by none other than Buster-15. "I have heard of Dab Tabmow. They say you are half man, half Cricket, and talk like a Bearman, and are as accurate as a Dnooblian. Is this true?"

"Yep, buddy," says Dab Tabmow.

"What the heck are all those pistons for?" asks Mutant Boy.

"The snarlbeasts. You see, they communicate by barking. The quality of the sound does not matter. It is all about the beat. We are pounding out the snarlbeast death rhythm. They will not come into the valley if the valley warns of death! Now we must get back to pulling our chains before the next cycle begins. It is a very long and complex set of cross rhythms."

Dab Tabmow and Mutant Boy follow the young Crickets to their piston tower.

"Gosh Dab Tabmow, you didn't even flinch at that spear! Didn't it scare you?" asks Mutant Boy.

"No."

"Whatever…" replies Mutant Boy as he whacks at vegetation with his buzz saw hand.

They get to the piston tower where the young Crickets give Dab Tabmow and Mutant Boy some ear plugs. There's one leftover earplug. Dab Tabmow reverts to Bearman mode.

"Hey buddy, that's quite a contraption you got there," he yells. "Do you have to do this twenty-nine/six?"

"No, Master Tabmow. The snarlbeasts only come in the day. We work in shifts all day, but we can sleep at night. It is easier when the wind blows and we only have to control the rhythm. But on a calm day like today, we toil mightily."

"How many beasts are there?" asks Mutant Boy.

"We can hear the barks of many in the distance, but we think only the same three come around here."

"Hey, buddy, I think I know what your problem is, and I think Mutant Boy and I can solve it for you."

"What, Master? What?!" asks Mutant Boy.

"Follow."

Mutant Boy rolls his eye.

Dab Tabmow says, "MULTI-VISION TORNADO ATTACK, LEVEL 10!" And he spins out of the valley and into the hills.

Mutant Boy shakes his head and spins his hands and feet into buzz saw wheels. He scoots out of the valley after Dab Tabmow. As they travel, the barking of snarlbeasts gets louder.

Mudhosh paused it. "Dluhosh, I bet he got the idea of Mutant Boy sprinting on buzz saws from Dnooblian sprinting! Trukk-9 is a genius. I plan to work for him someday."

The sound of snarlbeasts woke up Miles. "KILL KILL KILL," he yelled. Then he said, "Oh, jeez, this part... Might as well go back to sleep, Miles." Miles jumped down to look for the snarlbeasts. He found his tennis ball instead and gave it a good thrashing.

Mudhosh pressed play again.

The scene switches to Dab Tabmow and Mutant Boy pulling up to a giant quaint picket-fenced house that sits on top of a hill. There are snarlbeasts barking from inside the house. Seemingly fearless, Dab Tabmow knocks on the door. Mutant Boy keeps his buzz saws going.

Heavy footfalls from within the house cause the patio furniture to shift away from the wall. The door flies open and a humanoid Giant looks down at Dab Tabmow. "What do you want?"

"Hey, buddy, I thought you'd like to know that your snarlbeasts have been getting out and terrorizing a community of Crickets down in the valley."

The snarlbeasts bark rhythmically from behind a heavy wooden door that seems about to pop off its hinges. They bark in their THREAT rhythm, which sounds very scary over the new speaker system that Mudhosh bought with his own money on Chuffed-18.

Miles hid under Dluhosh's bed.

Mutant Boy keeps his buzz saws going. The Giant addresses him now. "Take it easy there little guy. Why don't you folks come in for tea and we can talk about this?"

Mutant Boy senses a trap and lunges at the Giant with all buzz saws on full RPM. Dab Tabmow puts him into a headlock and says, "We'd be happy to have tea with you, buddy."

"Well come on in. Don't mind the snarlbeasts. Here, let me stack some books on your chairs for you. Can you climb up there? Good." The Giant brings them each a biscuit the size of a manhole cover. "Do you take milk and sugar?"

"Yes, please."

"My snarlbeasts don't go out at night. The fraidy-cats are scared of the dark. I have to leave a nightlight on and a clock ticking under their bed. And in the day they are out in the yard sometimes, but I don't think they go far. How much damage have they done? I'm so sorry..."

"Yep, that is consistent with the schedule reported by the Crickets. And they say that the snarlbeasts have eaten dozens over the past several years."

"Oh my. What can I do to compensate them? Insectoids are people too..." says the contrite humanoid Giant.

The scene cuts to a great celebration. The Giant and the Crickets, including all of Dee's teens as extras, share a picnic at the Giant's house. Some Cricket children ride the snarlbeasts around the Giant's hill while others bounce on a trampoline the size of a four-lane roundabout. It is the first day in their living memory that they aren't pulling chain in the daytime.

Mudhosh turned it off and Miles came back in.

Miles said, "Dude, those snarlbeasts totally look like two guys in a suit. You got pantomime snarlbeasts, visible wires on the trampoline Crickets, and terrible artifacting around the green screen projections. It's nothing but cheapness. And, c'mon man, the Crickets are NOT going to befriend snarlbeasts just like that. Besides, the little guy is supposed to SLAY the Giant, not have tea with him."

"Go lie down!" said Mudhosh.

Poor Miles went to curl up on his smelly old couch.

"I've seen a lot of Earthling television too, Mudhosh, and the guys have a point. Even Trukk-9 was blown away by the quality. But I think the Dab Tabmow show is possibly more important than anything on Earth TV, regardless of the cheapness of the special effects."

Do I believe in a higher power? Yes, I have met one or two. I am not that impressed.
~ O'Buzznid-3

ULBTX REUNION

This time it was ULBTX-123 who waited for his friend ULBTX-404 on the outskirts of the Upper Left Buttocks Region of the dark matter Great Hologram.

404 wasn't late, but 123 was desperate for a sympathetic ear, so had arrived early.

Finally 404 popped up and said, "Hey 123, how are you these days?"

404 knew that things had been bad for his old friend lately. He had heard gossip from other Pixel People through the grapevine.

"I'm sure you've heard I'm on academic probation, and I'm sure you know how unjust it is," said 123.

404 knew where this conversation was headed, so he tried to change the subject. "Sometimes a guy can really get the shaft. But hey, I brought you an extra big load of CO2 and a few metric tons of that methane I've been promising. This should be pretty helpful, huh?"

"Yeah, I suppose I should keep up with the climate change program, but I no longer have the grants to fund monitoring. Earth is going to shit right on schedule and I can't even watch. Those FOOLS on the Chancellery! What do they know?!"

"They are pretty old and set in their ways…" replied 404. "But hey, did I tell you that I fixed the problem of my pumpkinheaded humanoid planet. Boy, it sure took a lot of work, but I was able to genetically re-engineer the next generation's genome back to normal. It's kind of amusing to observe. The females' pumpkinhead-adapted birth canals are kind of loose, so babies tend to slide right out. They've adapted by strategically placing foam pads on their shoes. I think they have a lot of potential in their naturally-evolved condition, actually."

"You think that's a lot of work… Check this out. I lose my tenure if I don't clean up ninety percent of my pixel's space-time wrinkles. That's right! Nothing but scrubbing space for decades! Thank you Chancellors! Bastards! I'm on the verge of proving the greatest discovery of all time. They are just jealous. They can't accept that a minor Pixel Person out here in the Upper Left Buttocks Region has answered the question of questions. They know that I have conclusively proven that a humanoid race with big enough feet can rise to become our creator! They can't handle it!"

"Well, 123, I have reviewed your work very carefully and I think you are definitely onto something. If you would allow me, I think I have some ideas to help tweak the statistical analysis," offered 404.

"Thanks, but I have it under control, 404. You know what they accused me of?"

"Um, I really couldn't say…"

"They say that I suffer from an advanced case of confirmation bias! Confirmation bias!? They say that I'm using my hypotheses to validate my data, and then using that data to support my hypotheses. They say my theory is built on faulty conclusions like a house of cards! How ridiculous is that?!"

"That would be pretty ridiculous," replied 404.

"And that attitude tells me all I need to know right there. They know I'm right, so they are putting up a roadblock because they can't handle the truth. Now I'm more sure of the truth than ever! And if they can't see the TRUTH, I'm going to hit them with it right there in their ivory bellybutton!"

"Um, what do you have in mind?"

"Don't tell anyone, but I just need to push things a little – just a little. If the Chancellors don't believe my theoretical conclusions, then I'll give them the real conclusion! Then they'll see the truth!"

"Okay, 123, I don't think you need to tell me any more. Here's your supply of greenhouse gases. I'll see if I can meet you back here again next month, but I'll probably be pretty busy about then," explained 404.

The two old friends gave a half-hearted Upper Left Buttocks brotherhood chant and went their separate ways.

ULBTX-123 dumped his greenhouse gasses into Earth's atmosphere. He wasn't as careful as he normally was. He just picked an arbitrary spot that happened to be over the European Union somewhere and off-gassed the whole load.

Even the toughest piece of leather can be chewed into a pudding.
By a Cricket, at least.
~ O'Buzznid-3

DLUHOSH'S ARRIVAL MOTHER ROOST

Dluhosh's ship exited the final wormhole on route to Mother Roost. He and Mudhosh could see the planet on the viewer. But all Miles/Michael/Gregory could see was Miles' inner thigh.

"Hey, throw some bacon at the viewer so we can see too!"

Mudhosh replicated some churdle bacon and threw it. Miles bounded like a little steeplechase runner over Mudhosh's control panel, swallowed the bacon whole, and went back to licking his empty scrotum.

"Did you guys get a look at it?" asked Dluhosh.

"Was it that bluish dot in the center?"

"Yep, that was it."

"So what's the plan, Dluhosh?" asked Mudhosh.

"Let's have a look at their TV for signs that the battleship crew from the Earth invasion has been captured."

They tuned in to the news. It was happy squabs with a brand new orphanage, coverage of a bake-off, a new world record in skate flying, a show about traditional banjo picking, the latest model of hybrid hovercraft, etcetera.

"Well nothing here indicates that there's been a recent alien invasion, so ULBTX-123 is probably just blowing hot air again," said Dluhosh. "I'm thinking that I'd like to check in on a couple of old friends – some of the ones I showed you in the video clips. Hopefully Muffin Hen is still doing her thing – I just want to see and maybe get some pictures for Pip-The-Blue. Then I think we should go look for Dayv. Hopefully he's at his cabin. We should abduct him and re-plant his old memory. He's a great guy, and he seems like the type who would know the rivers and beaches – could get us started on some likely fossil collecting locations."

***

Sure enough, Muffin Hen was in her kitchen baking. Dluhosh noticed a couple of new muffin trophies and ribbons on the living room shelves.

They flew to Dayv's place. They approached from inland and found several small hovercrafts parked around the cabin.

"Hmm… Looks like he has company. Do you see anyone?"

"No sapient life signs in the cabin," replied Mudhosh.

They flew to the beach beyond the meadow and forest where Dluhosh figured Dayv was surfing. The first oddity they noticed was what appeared to be a small PLUMBOB-issue flying saucer towing a Dung Beetle into a large wave breaking over an offshore reef. Several other insectoids and a few large shaggy Roostians straddled their boards and looked to be cheering the Dung Beetle.

Dluhosh stopped his ship. "What the…?" he said.

"Oh boy, Dluhosh, I thought you said…"

"I did. Something is very wrong. What is PLUMBOB doing here, and why are they interacting with the locals? And all those insectoids? That's way too many for that one little saucer. I think we found…"

"Uh, Dluhosh, I have something interesting on the scanner. Pull up a little. It appears to be a large hub of antimatter and advanced technology. Right down there…"

They pulled up to the edge of the forest over the beach and saw the Battleship Aedeagus resting there at the top of the beach. A Moth technician was using the ship's grabber beam to gather firewood. There was a well-established camp around the high edge of the saucer, and the plants of the forest appeared to have grown right up into the main port and onto the ship's bridge.

"Yep, that's a full-on Galactic Mountain Melter. This is what ULBTX-123 did with the ship that melted your mountain, guys. I can't believe he just left the whole ship right out here in the open."

Mudhosh threw some bacon so the guys could see what they were talking about.

Miles said, "I wonder what that big voice asshole was thinking. That doesn't exactly look like punishment. That guy is definitely too careless to be a scientist."

"We can't abduct Dayv right now, but we should get the Moths to tell us what's going on. Grab those guys, place them under a dome, and hit them with some calming agent. Do you think you can handle that, Mudhosh?"

"Like a rogue Dnooblian!"

Mudhosh pulled the grabber beams in like he was sucking a couple of strands of spaghetti. The Moths flopped up and down, smacking the top and then the bottom of Dluhosh's ship a couple of times each as they came through the port. They couldn't feel the impacts through the grabber beams, but it must have been a disorienting ride.

At first the two Moths panicked under the dome. They shed a lot of scales as they flew around within the confined space. They looked like they were in a psychedelic snow globe. Once the calming agent had taken effect, they sat looking at the Dnooblians and the little animal who was yelling KILL at them.

"Hi," said one of the Moths.

"Hi. What's going on here?" asked Dluhosh.

"It is a long story," replied one of the Moths. "I am a second technician aboard the Battleship Aedeagus, and this is the third technician. We found ourselves stranded here after beginning our mission on a planet called Dirt – we know not how. Our radio, engine, weapons and cloaking device are all mysteriously disconnected from the power system. Those Dirtlings have got some kind of space-time super weapon. We were discovered by these locals and, to be honest, I have a feeling that Captain Spotty is in no hurry to be rescued."

"It's EARTH, not Dirt!" barked Miles.

Dluhosh said, "Yeah, we know about the mountain melting – we were there. They are from that planet." He pointed a tentacle at Miles.

"They?"

"Yeah, there are three of us in here, and we are all Earthlings, so watch out," said Miles.

"Really? You are the Earthlings? Not exactly what I expected, but, yeah, I think Captain Spotty is finally convinced that we shouldn't be messing with you anymore."

"And what about that PLUMBOB ship? When did they arrive?" asked Dluhosh.

"Oh yeah, I guess it has been a few weeks. They are a couple of Crickets. They told us they were lost in space. The Captain is not that interested in asking a lot of questions these days, so he invited them to hang out. Those two guys can shred though – the one with the sponge is a drop-knee king. And best of all, they figured out that they could use a grabber beam to tow a surfer into big waves that move too fast to paddle into."

Miles said, "They tow-in surf on Earth too. They have little jet-boaty things instead of flying saucers, but it's basically the same deal."

"You know about this surfing activity too? You?" asked the third technician.

"Oh yeah man, I used to boogie board all the time before I hurt my neck. I can shred a little bit," said Miles as he chased his tail – first to the left, and then to the right.

"You? This I have to see."

"My neck, man – I wish I could…"

"WHOA! Did you see that move?" asked the other Moth technician. "Dunger pulled a gorf off that big barreling section! Did you see that? And he's still going!"

"I saw that," said Miles. "Now let me get this straight. Because I'm not from around here and stuff, you know. Did I just see a gigantic Dung Beetle rip that close-out pitch? Throw some bacon Mudhosh! And now that's a feathered dinosaur on a longboard being towed by a flying saucer into that big A-frame? Right? Dluhosh, calming agent please! Miles needs calming agent!"

"Miles looks fine to me," said Dluhosh. "Now gentlemen, I think we also owe you an explanation. When do you think your captain will be available?"

***

Around the campfire, Dluhosh told his story.

"I am a rogue Dnooblian, but I was once a PLUMBOB agent. I did the original investigation here on Mother Roost – been a couple of years ago now, and I was never able to finish my report. But I recall my encounter with Dayv as one of the highlights of my career."

"Yowza! I'm telling you – there ain't no getting away from a cat like Dluhosh once he gets after you!" said Dayv. "He may be a little cat, but he threw me ten feet through the air and wrestled my hovercraft out from under me! Respect, brother." They did a wing/tentacle bump.

Dluhosh flashed blue and continued. "Then I was sent to Earth, like you, on a politically motivated bogus mission. Griffer-1 is bound and determined to get Earth into the Galactic Pool. I can see why politically he would want it, but Earth seems a little too dangerous and unpredictable to be messing with."

"That's right. You mess with us – we mess with you," said Miles, scooting his bottom through the beach grass. "So you don't EVEN want to start anything."

"It was Griffer-1 himself who got me out of stasis. He made it sound like your planet was a sleepy blue and green paradise that just needed waking up," said Captain Spotty.

Miles replied from down on the beach, where he was now rolling on something dead. "That guy is lame!"

"Anyway," continued Dluhosh. "I crashed, was sheltered by Michael and Gregory, and was eventually rescued. But after my lousy experience with Planet One politics, I went rogue and stayed on Earth. It really is a fascinating study there – you wouldn't believe some of the crazy stuff they get up to. Anyway, I was still there when you guys melted Mount Rushmore. I grabbed these guys for their protection and gave them a tour of Dnooblia and Chuffed-18. Along the way we've gotten up to some roguish behavior and have pirated some useful technology.

"That is quite a story," said Captain Spotty. "I would be interested in hearing more – especially any news from home."

"During my short return, I noticed things changing in the Galactic Pool, Captain. I think you'd be impressed. And you probably haven't read O'Buzznid-3's memoir. He talks about you in it, Captain. His words have carried a lot of weight back home. I can loan you my ereader if you'd like to read it."

"Yes, please. So old Buzzy wrote a memoir… That rascal. I hope he does not spill too much about our days in the academy. He completed his life cycle then, correct?"

"Yes. In fact he tricked a Bearman into raising his grubs," said Dluhosh.

"So all of them probably survived... Buzzy was always a bit of a rebel. But, huh, Crickets being raised by a Bearman... Interesting."

"You might also like to see a television show that Trukk-9 produces. It's a superhero martial arts series starring a half-man, half-Cricket character."

"They allow Trukk-9 on television?" asked Captain Spotty.

"Yep. Thanks to my friends here, the President decreed a new TV network with five-HUNDRED channels."

"That was my idea," said Miles.

"All of Trukk-9's underground cinema material has its own channel – even all of his early shorts and documentaries. To me, his Dab Tabmow show seems to be part of a cultural shift. We'll show you some episodes. The over-all theme is that insectoids are people too, and the young people of all species across the Galactic Pool seem okay with that idea."

"I will have to see that to believe it," said the Dung Beetle.

Captain Spotty and his crew stared into the dying campfire with their thoughts.

"Captain, I think my friends and I can get your ship repaired. And with any luck, we might be able to get you home a lot faster than you'd think. One of our pirated pieces of technology is what we call a super wormhole. It's very fickle, however."

"That would be nice, but…" Captain Spotty looked at the faces of his crew. "But I think the men somewhat enjoy this lifestyle. Perhaps we are not in a big hurry…"

Dluhosh replied. "Okay, we'd like to have a little adventure ourselves while we are here, Captain. But let me know when you are ready and I'll see what I can do. By the way, Dayv, I was hoping you could help us find some likely fossil locations nearby. "

"I normally don't pay much attention to dead things I can't eat, daddy-o, but what would it look like where these things be?" said Dayv.

"We'd be looking for exposed rock, perhaps in sea cliffs, mountainsides, deserts or river valleys maybe, where the rock has layers visible in it or little nodules poking out," said Dluhosh.

The Bee engineer jumped up and said, "I think I know just what you need. I have seen something a lot like that during my afternoon flights up a river near here. Let me show you where." He then did a little figure-eight dance and shook his abdomen as he described the coordinates of what he thought would be a good place to try for fossils.

***

A couple of nights later, Captain Spotty and Doctor Exoskeleton shared a mug of raw Roostian millet beer in the Captain's quarters.

"So, Exoskeleton, did you ever meet O'Buzznid-3?"

"I have heard of him, certainly. But I never had the pleasure."

"We entered the academy together at the start of the war. He was too short to be a pilot, but he was a great commander – ended up in charge of the Tiger Beetles in the ground defense. We used to get together when our leave coincided. One night we were out at a club and some Blister Beetles started giving him the business."

"Uh, oh."

"Yeah, we had drained a few repli-meads and Buzzy turns to them and says, 'Suck my intromittent organ.'"

"Good one!"

"Old Buzzy had some zingers, alright. Anyway, the biggest Blister Beetle says, 'If I could find it, little Cockroach.'"

"Ouch!"

"Yeah, Buzzy hated being called that. But before I can stop him, he has that big old Blister Beetle in a headlock and is kicking him in the spiracles." Captain Spotty stood up to demonstrate. "Then he takes him under the labial palp and flips him onto his elytra. I had never seen Buzzy in tarsus-to-tarsus combat, but boy that Blister Beetle was even more surprised than me. So, of course, the guy's friends all pile on. Long story short, we end up in the medical unit and spend a week in the brig. We never had any trouble from Blister Beetles again though."

"I should guess not."

"Well, Exoskeleton, are you ready to go back to Planet One and be a faceless bureaucrat locked in a stasis box again?"

"I have to admit it – I do miss my queen. But I also have to admit that I feel like a whole new man living here. It feels – I do not know – like maybe it is supposed to be this way. Is this like it was before the war, Spotty?"

"It has been so long that it is hard to recall. But, yes, we did have freedom and time for recreation. I like what Buzzy has done. He realized that guys like me and him are the last connection to our former glory. I think his book must be opening a lot of eyes…" Captain Spotty's voice trailed off and he took another swig of millet beer.

"And you…?"

"And I feel like I should be doing the same, Exoskeleton. How many of us are left? There is a quote in Buzzy's book. 'Count not the number who remain, but measure the size of the periviceral sinus of the last one standing.' And I cannot help but think that this quote was directed at me, my friend."

"And if the Dnooblian is right?"

"If the Dnooblian is right… If he is right – if things are changing, and just need a little bit of a nudge in the right direction – then it might occur to one that one has a Galactic Class Mountain Melter at one's disposal…"

***

As the guys scanned a dry riverbed for clues of fossils, Dluhosh asked, "It didn't seem too much like I was trying to start a revolution or foment a coup the other night, did it?"

"Dluhosh, no, it didn't seem to me like you tried hard enough. I kept wanting to yell 'Go start a coup you big warship captain!' You were just beating around the bush."

"Really? You think it's okay for us to get involved in affairs of state?"

"Dluhosh, the point of going rogue isn't just so you can cruise around looking for fossils and befriending alien puppy dogs. If that were the case, it wouldn't be illegal, right? You are SUPPOSED to go around causing trouble for causes you believe in. I think you should come up with a plan and convince Captain Spotty. Be direct. None of this hint dropping nonsense. It's unbecoming of a rogue Dnooblian. There, I said it."

By sheer luck, Miles had been looking in the direction of the fossil scanner.

"Hey! What's that?" he said.

Dluhosh stopped the ship. Sticking out of a cut bank on the river was the end of a femur. The ball of the femur where it would have attached to the creature's hip was the size of a fully inflated Dnooblian pufferfish. The guys also noticed several large brown vertebrae scattered around on the gravel bar downstream.

Mudhosh lowered Dluhosh and Miles onto the fossil site. Dluhosh obtained a full scan of the area and examined it.

"The skull is buried in that bank. It's not a complete skeleton, but it's enough. Wow, the teeth are the size of gbananas! The scanner dates this rock at fifty-million years. So this is a dinosaur species that probably evolved here on Mother Roost. This dinosaur would not be a known species on Earth."

Miles was very excited about the new dinosaur even though he seemed more interested in whatever had dug the small hole under one of the vertebrae. "I would propose that this species be named after Dluhosh! Is it okay if Gregory and I write up the official description? From the looks of it, we might have discovered *Tyrannosaurus dluhoshi*!"

At the sound of that exclamation coming from Miles, a small feathered lizard-like animal bit him on the nose. Miles jumped back and tried to run away. The lizard chased him down the creek bed until Miles ducked behind a boulder. The lizard scampered over the boulder and launched itself into the air. Its ribs stuck out to form a kind of wing, and its stiff tail feathers spread out to give it additional control. The lizard glided upwards at a steep angle and then turned to dive at Miles.

Dluhosh grabbed the animal from the air in mid dive with his hunting tentacles. "Wow! What a neat little animal," he said. "He was going to teach you a lesson!"

Miles said, "KILL KILL KILL!"

And then Miles said, "That's a badass little dinosaur! That's officially the coolest thing ever. Although I'm not sure that ol' Miles thinks so, you know. Let me check that out."

But when Dluhosh tried to show it to Miles, he growled and bared his teeth. So Dluhosh took some pictures and let the animal go.

***

Dluhosh took his ship into orbit. He uncloaked and released a tachyon plasma jet in bursts at a regular interval. Within seconds, the headless torso avatar of ULBTX-123 revolved in front of the ship's viewing panel.

"What do you want now?!" said a very big voice.

"Sorry to disturb you ULBTX-123. We know you are busy scrubbing space, and we don't want to take up your precious time. But we have a proposition."

"What could you possibly have that I would want?"

"We have a way to get rid of Planet One's conniving politicians once and for all."

"Where have I heard that before? Silly ammonite, you are wasting my time. Go away before I feed you to my dinosaurs!"

"Okay, but the last time we attacked Planet One, all we had was three pseudo-superhero Earthlings with feet that obviously weren't big enough. This time we have a Galactic Class Mountain Melter, a Captain of the Fleet, and hard evidence of multiple felonies committed by the Vice President."

"Felonies smelonies. And anyone can destroy mountains. Forget it," said ULBTX-123.

"You see, we don't actually want you to fix the ship's weapon systems. The captain is only willing to bluff."

"Hold it. Do you reference the ship that I threw to my dinosaurs?"

"Yes."

"I hate to disappoint you, but my dinosaurs have torn that ship apart by now, and the crew are either imprisoned or eaten. So there goes your plan."

"Your dinosaurs are smart enough to recognize the importance of alien contact. You chose some very good ones when you brought them here so long ago. In reality, they have become great friends with the insectoids. Go figure," said Dluhosh.

"How are their feet?"

"Very big. And claws like you wouldn't believe... You would be proud. Heck, you SHOULD be proud. And you know what would be really cool?"

"What?"

"Another one of your really awesome meteors…"

"You liked that last time? Pretty scary stuff for you insignificant pip-squeaks, huh?"

"Oh, yes. Just dreadful. Planet One is still talking about it," replied Dluhosh.

"I have an even better trick this time. But those two punks you sometimes travel with – they're not coming, are they?"

"Nope. I killed them," said Dluhosh. "Blew their cocky asses away. Plasma jet. You should have seen it. It was magnificent."

Miles said, "HEY!"

"They had it coming," said ULBTX-123.

"Damn right, huh Mudhosh?"

"Oh yeah, those guys were filthy and smelly and they thought they were better than everyone. Plus they had no aesthetic sense, and they played with themselves constantly," said Mudhosh.

"Alright, I could use a distraction from the scrubbing. What do I have to do?"

"Simple. You repair the battleship's engines, cloaking device, and radio. Then you take us where we need to go. I promise that it won't require more than two additional wormholes, and there are hardly any in that sector anyway. I'd think you wouldn't even need to clean them up. I see it as very low risk on your part."

"And so I get to throw a meteor down on their asses?"

"Sure, sure, but just an atmospheric graze, right?" asked Dluhosh.

"Oh, alright…" said ULBTX-123. "But I don't want to reveal myself to the others. I'm much too important for them. Do not mention me by name."

"It's a deal then. There's no need to reveal you to the other parties. I'll come up with an explanation for everything, and I've already been careful to cover you up. I've just been explaining you as pirated technology that Mudhosh and I acquired on a raid."

"Good. I like that. I am a sort of pirate, aren't I? 'Pirate ULBTX-123' has a nice ring to it. ULBTX-123, Space Pirate…"

Mudhosh said, "I'd drop the confusing part and go with something like Space Pirate-123."

Miles said, "I think you should go with Space Poodle Zero."

"Hush little animal! I do not like you. You remind me of someone…"

"I have it! You should go with Space Pirate-X!" said Mudhosh.

"Yep, that really works on you," said Dluhosh. "It's an excellent alias. No one will ever suspect it's you. So, please, Space Pirate-X, first begin by fixing the battleship. And remember – no weapons."

***

Captain Spotty gave Dluhosh a tour of the Battleship Aedeagus.

"You were right, Dluhosh. Everything but the weapon is back online."

The Bee engineer trailed behind with his head hung low. For he believed that he had failed somehow.

"I have to tell you," said Dluhosh. "It's just lucky that I happened to steal this repair technology from a pirate space cruiser. And even then, there's no way we would have been able to repair those power couplings if your engineer hadn't used his quantum cauterizer on them. In fact, had the gaps been left as is, it may have eventually caused your ship to be sucked into an alternate dimension."

"Funny, that is what we assumed really had happened," said Captain Spotty. He gave the Bee a friendly punch in the trochanter.

"We still have the question of your local friends here. It would be easier to just wipe their memories and leave, but I think we might consider leaving it up to them," said Dluhosh.

Captain Spotty regarded Dluhosh. "Seems like they may already be in the Galactic Pool by default..."

Dluhosh added, "They'd probably win in the vote anyway..."

The Captain whispered, "Having them along would help keep the men's morale up..."

Dluhosh turned a deeper shade of blue and said, "Could let THEM decide if they even want a vote..."

The Captain peeped, "Most democratic way..."

Dluhosh whispered, "Huh?"

The Captain, in a slightly louder peep, said, "It's the most democratic way..."

Dluhosh cupped a tentacle around his beak and hissed, "I think they would also make a very friendly addition to the Galactic Assembly..."

The Captain drew a Cricket smiley face in the dust on his control panel.

Dluhosh added a Dnooblian beak to it.

And then in the most booming voice he could make, Captain O'Spotnid-3, Cricket Captain of the Fleet said, "Yes Dluhosh, we will surf!"

And they surfed.

(Dluhosh and Mudhosh were, of course, very good at it.)

***

The next morning, after one last dawn patrol surf session, everyone of alien origin packed up their stuff and boarded their ships. Dayv and 'Blood' came along for the ride – with Captain Spotty on the Aedeagus. The men collected a few final plants and found room for them in the short forest that the bridge had become.

"Captain, O'Hecknid and O'Jecknid – follow me into orbit. Hopefully I'll be able to engage the super wormhole on the first try," said Dluhosh.

"Dluhosh," said Captain Spotty, "I would like to call someone first now that my quantum radio is working. Just a personal call – it will only take a second."

"Sure thing, Captain."

Captain Spotty picked up the microphone and said, "Dispatch, this is the Battleship Aedeagus. Can you read me?"

After a moment's delay, a voice replied. "Did you say the Aedeagus? Is this Captain O'Spotnid-3? It's really you?"

"Yes, but I would like to speak with the regular dispatcher please."

"This is she, darling. I'm so excited – where have you…?"

"No, you do not understand. She is a Cricket. A Cricket with a beautiful smile…"

"Oh, Spotty! It's me! It's me!"

"You are not her. You spoke on official airwaves using a contraction!"

"Oh, yes, yes. I mean no. I mean, don't worry Captain baby. You've been gone so long... There's a new law that says we can speak with contractions now. Plus, by a weird quirk in the law, we are also now allowed to use contraptions. You should see this one I just got. My microphone stand is now on a little plastic base that lets me flip…" She goes silent for a second. "…button and it pops back up again."

"It really is you. I'm coming home! I have a couple of errands to run and then I'm coming straight to see you. Don't mention this to anyone yet though, sweet-heart. And please save your appetite because I'm getting itchy and I don't plan to go back into stasis ever again."

The ultimate satisfaction is in knowing you did your best. But what I really like is when the lazy stuff turns out good.
~ O'Buzznid-3

FISHING ON SWAMPY-12

Jimmy and his production team had tried to discourage the President. They explained that the production called for pure down-home traditional fishing on Swampy-12. There would be no hovering medical ship, no sandwiches, and they'd be sleeping in tents out on the swamp. But the more they tried to discourage him, the more he wanted to go. They really did try.

***

Slee-12 was a middle-aged Swamp Master, so he stood approximately twenty-five feet tall and was bright yellow. His boat, a barge named Old Black, was one-hundred feet long and twenty feet wide. Slee kept his fishing tackle in ammo boxes.

Slee's instructions were to simply give Jimmy and his production crew a fishing-show's-worth of reality and excitement. If Slee's show was selected, it would premier in prime time during Swamp Master Heritage Week.

"G'day folks! Welcome to Slee's Eelin' Hole! I have a couple of special guests today, mates. With me are none-other than Jimmy Fresneaux and President of the Galactic Pool, Gren Wee-1!"

Jimmy and the President waved at the camera.

"Now you might ask yourself, 'What are big-wigs like these doing with ol' Slee down in the swamp?' Well, ol' Slee has the opportunity to hit the galactic airwaves! That's right! If I can put some fat eels in the boat for my friends here, you might be able to catch me in a time-slot next to Jimmy's Fishin' Hole. I have to admit, I'm a bit nervous, but let's get started, shall we?"

Slee passed out ear muffs and fired up the jet engine on the back of Old Black. They sounded like they were rocketing across the swamp, but they were actually making only about five knots. Jimmy's producer/director liked the visual though. She had them take several passes in front of the Swampy-12 sunrise. Jimmy and the President didn't like it as much. Even at only five knots, the dense clouds of bugs soon formed a pasty crust on the sweaty skin of Jimmy, and infested the tabby fur of the President.

When they stopped, Slee jumped in the swamp, washed off, and secreted a new layer of slime. He looked at Jimmy and the President and apologized.

After wiping off most of the bugs, Jimmy asked, "Slee, what would you say the advantages and disadvantages are in being a twenty-five-foot-tall bright yellow fisherman?"

"Yes, Jimmy, I'd say it's very much an advantage. The eels and I can see each other better that way, right off the bat."

The President had a more confused look than normal. "You WANT them to see you?"

"Yup. They are a very curious beastie, Mister President. That jet engine isn't providing any thrust to the boat to speak of. It just mimics the mating call of the male eel. The sound attracts rival males and ripe females."

"But what is propelling these boats?" asked Jimmy.

"Oh, sorry, I have very fine teams of armored catfish that I should introduce you to. Come up front and take a gander!"

The President and Jimmy saw the dorsal fins of a team of eight white stallion armored catfish glowing through the murky swamp water. Slee tapped the side of the boat and the team rose to the surface. Their eyeballs were on top of their heads and elongated upwards like little periscopes, allowing them to see above water.

"HOOOEEEE!" said Jimmy. "Man alive, boy howdy, and everything! Now those are some serious catfish you got there Slee!"

"Yup, they make a fine team and they are as friendly as can be. You can swim with them back at the corral later if you like."

"Definitely," said the director. "We'll get some underwater footage as well."

"Um, okay, I guess," said Jimmy.

"So everybody, I stopped in this location because I saw some motion in the weeds over yonder, and a sizable boil behind us over there. I think we may have stumbled upon a mating pair, or possibly rival males. In either case they will likely see us as a threat, which puts them in a biting mood."

"Let me ask you a question about branding, Slee. You have a lot of real estate on your body there – you ever think about logos?"

"Yup. I could hold a lot of sponsorship logos on a body this big. Unfortunately, the slime precludes clothing. But watch this!"

Slee pushed a button with his foot and two small spotlights on either side of the boat flicked on. The lights projected logo images of a Slee's Eel Slammer on his chest and a Slee's Eelin' Stick on his back.

Jimmy was very impressed and said so.

"And that's some top quality eelin' gear right there, mate! Let me show you how to use it."

Slee tied his lure onto a braided rope that hung from the end of his pole. The line was wound onto a Slee's Really Real Steel Eel Reel as big as an oil drum. The rod was more like a utility pole than a fishing pole.

"Alright, Jimmy. The idea is to cast this bad boy as far as you can away from the boat. Don't try to cast it at an eel close by, like you would on a boiling bass. Always cast it as far as you can. My quackless duck patterned Slee's Eel Slammer is sure to get their attention way out on the perimeter."

"Slee, that lure is as big as an outboard motor! And where are the hooks?" asked Jimmy.

"Hooks? No hooks needed, mate! Watch this."

Slee cast his lure and it arced across the sky. The lure landed with a huge splash about three-hundred feet away.

The camera zoomed into the lure.

"Now I like to let the Slee's Eel Slammer rest on the surface until all the ripples die down. Then I give it a twitch…"

The swamp water bulged up and the lure disappeared with a great sucking sound. The back of a twenty-foot eel snaked across the surface of the swamp away from the boat.

Slee shouted, "FIRE IN THE HOLE!" and the eel's massive head exploded - sending eel head shrapnel and beautiful bright blue blood across the swamp as far as the eye could see. The concussion caused the team of catfish to rear up on their caudal fins.

"WOOOO! That's a good one!" shouted Slee. He looked over at Jimmy and the President. "Oops," he said.

Steve slimed off his smattering of eel blood and brains, and was as good as new. He turned on a pump and tried to squirt Jimmy off with swamp water. He could see it wasn't helping. He hung his great big head.

They cleaned up as best as they could. The President optimistically rigged up a Chompy Chunkbait, but he flubbed the knot and dropped the lure over the side. He leaned over the rail to try and spot the lure in the murk.

"Now that commotion should bring the second eel closer. We might get us a double. So whatever you do, don't get too close to the water. An angry eel can suck the spots off a swamp roo…"

Before Slee could finish, a head with a mouth big enough to swallow half a man erupted from the water and swallowed half of the President. The alpha armored catfish of Slee's team turned and rammed the eel in the side. The eel disgorged the President back into the boat, minus his fur from the waist up. He had also lost his hat, his new sponsorship jersey, and his Basses Glasses with the custom braided and branded lanyard.

The Discreet Service agents administered first aid and calming agent, and the director feigned concern as she reviewed the priceless footage of the President being sucked nude by an eel.

Poor Slee thought he had blown his big chance.

The Discreet Service group captain said, "The President is delirious and is drifting in and out of consciousness. We need to get him to a medical probaluator. Fast!"

Slee said, "There's only one way to get there faster." He unhitched his alpha stallion, grabbed the President under his arm, straddled the great armored fish, and rode toward the marina first aid station at six knots.

The rest of the catfish instinctively followed their leader.

***

The marina nurse explained. "I've had to sedate him for his own good. Whatever happened to him out there seems to have deeply traumatized him. When conscious, he springs his claws and thrashes about screaming. I am not authorized to erase the memory of a sitting President. He needs to be hospitalized on Planet One and remain sedated until lawyers can decide on his cure."

Slee said to the others, "I am so sorry. Dang, you are so nice to have given me a chance. And I blow it on the very first cast…"

The director said, "Are you kidding!? That was golden, Slee. What we just shot this morning is going to be a hit. It will be a great kick-off for the twelve-show first season that we want to sign you to. We need to get back out there for more action!"

"And son, I want to draw up a sponsorship package for you as soon as we have this show in the can!" added Jimmy.

"WOOOOO! It's eel on the barbi tonight!" said Slee.

Unfortunately, the excitement caused a small Swamp Master jubilee to break out on the dock. It was just Slee and a dozen spring break coeds, but Jimmy and the crew had to step back from the slime and wait until nature had run its course.

My mentor always said, 'Prior planning prevents piss-poor results.'
~ O'Buzznid-3

PLANNING ON CHUFFED-18

"Jacques, the first group of girls will be around in a few minutes. You know them all, and I'm making it easy on you by grouping them by name. These are all named Steence. Mother had a very good idea with this, Jacques, so we will be doing it a lot. I expect you to be here for these visits." Fleence pointed at a calendar. "Mondays, Wednesdays and Fridays, okay Jacques?"

"Aw, honey, does it hafta be Friday too? Sometimes that Friday afternoon bite turns on…"

"Jacques, what kind of father are you going to be if you don't even have time for the mothers? Besides, Jacques, they are all very pretty and they adore you."

"I know…" said Jimmy, scuffing at the floor with his silk slipper.

"They expect that you will imagine them in maternity denim over-alls, which is what they will be wearing. Can you handle that Jacques?"

"Yes, honey. I remember some of the Steences. They were very nice."

"Now please change into something that doesn't have logos on it, and take off your visor."

While Jimmy was changing, the first Steence showed up. She was about four months pregnant. The next two Steences to arrive shared the same age and clone line. They were both exactly seventy-nine days pregnant. The fourth pregnant Steence was a midwife, which was good because the fifth Steence was at full term.

Jimmy walked in wearing the leisure suit that Fleence had duplicated for him based on a picture from her PLUMBOB Earth archive. And he was drinking a Jimmy Juice from the gold goblet that she had given him for his birthday.

"Hi, Jimmy…" all the Steences said, waggling their fingers and smiling coyly at him.

"Hi, Steences, how's it goin'?" said Jimmy.

"Jacques has come up with names he'd like to suggest for your babies if they are boys. You are, of course, free to name your baby anything you want – but this loving gesture will help provide alternatives to Jimmy, Michael, Gregory, and Miles. Okay, Jacques, what would you love the first baby to be named?"

"Oh, sorry Fleence, I forgot… But I know some good names. Hold on. Okay," he pointed at the first Steence. "That one-"

"Jacques! Go whisper it to the baby, silly," said Fleence.

Jimmy put his goblet on the coffee table, knelt down in front of the Steence, and leaned in to her belly.

The Steence said, "Don't you want to feel him, Jimmy?"

Jimmy laid his hand on her belly and said, "If you are a boy, your name will be Skeeter."

"Oooh, that's pretty! Skeeter – I like that!" she said.

The other Steences said 'Skeeter' out loud and nodded their approval.

Jimmy walked on his knees to the next Steence. "And you shall be Gator."

"Oh, can my baby be Gator too?" said the identical 'twin' Steence. "I'm going to name her that even if she's a girl! It's so beautiful."

"Me too!" said the first identical Steence.

"Um, sure," said Jimmy.

"Tell the baby directly, okay?" she said.

Jimmy scooted over and put his lips to her belly. "Hello, little Gator."

Then to the midwife's baby bump he gave the name Rumpelstiltskin. She seemed very pleased.

Fleence said, "Jacques, can you tell us the meanings of these beautiful Earthling names, honey?"

"Oh, uh, probably… What was the first one again?"

"Skeeter," said the first Steence.

"Oh yeah, that's a good one. It means 'one with a penetrating… gaze'. And then Gator, right? It means 'one who is patient but explosive', and 'spinner of gold' is what Rumpelstiltskin means."

He moved over to the pregnantest of the Steences, glanced over at the kitchen, and said, "Your name will be… Fudge… Fudgy!"

"Fudgy?" asked Steence. "Oh, Jimmy – that would sound silly here. I don't know what it means where you are from, but 'fudge' is what we call a kind of chewy after-dinner treat.

"Ha ha, yeah, that would be silly. Okay… How about Lasagna then?"

"Ooh, yes! I LOVE it. It sounds very… very exotic!" She was so excited about the name Lasagna that her water broke.

Jimmy had to excuse himself for his six-o'clock appointment with a Beence-18, but he was back in time for the birth of little Lasagna-18, a seven-pound baby girl.

After her appointment, Beence-18 was still hanging around for all the excitement. She said to Jimmy, "I'm feeling optimistic, Jimmy. Can you give my zygote its name?"

"Your what?"

"My zygote. You know – the cell that's formed from the union of our gametes…?" said Beence.

"Oh, we don't have those words back on Earth. What was it again – Goat, what?"

"Zygote."

"I think Billy would be good," said Jimmy.

"Yay! I love Billy, Jimmy. It's lovely! Okay little Billy Zygote, let's go home. Thank you, Jimmy. You are very kind."

As Beence was leaving, Fleence's phone rang. "Hello. Uh huh, uh huh, oh boy… Dluhosh? Yes, we'll be right over."

"Jacques, honey, that was Mother, she said that Dluhosh has returned with something very important that he needs help with. Steence and Lasagna, you can rest here. We shouldn't be very long. Let's go Jacques!"

***

A planning meeting was in progress in the ballroom at the Kyleence-18/Trukk-9 estate on Chuffed-18. In attendance were:

The hosts,

Dluhosh, rogue Dnooblian,

Mudhosh, rogue Dnooblian (under containment dome),

Michael and Gregory in the forms of two babies and a wiener dog named Miles,

Dayv and 'Blood', blown-away feathered dinosaur surfers fresh from Mother Roost,

O'Hecknid-3 and O'Jecknid-3 – Bad-stuff specialist Crickets from PLUMBOB,

Captain O'Spotnid-3 of the Battleship Aedeagus,

'Dunger' the Dung Beetle navigator,

Doctor Exoskeleton,

The Bee engineer,

The Click Beetle pilot,

The second and third technician Moths,

Fleence-18 and Jacques "Jimmy" Fresneaux with their baby Lunker-18,

Dee-15, Bearman, purveyor of fine kittens, and cameraman extraordinaire,

Stick.E-5, plasmanoid, gaffer, sound engineer, and grabber beam magician,

and ULBTX-123, AKA Space Pirate-X.

Gregory banged his sippy-cup on the tray of his highchair and said, "I say we do it just like last time! These guys are big wimps. Just crash us through the window with a grabber beam and we'll take 'em down!"

Dluhosh said, "Well, Gregory, that didn't actually work last time, remember? We failed to stop the ship going to Earth. Plus, this time you are a baby with tiny little footsies."

Kyleence took control of the meeting. "Folks, recall that our goal is to make Griffer and Gro Skoo resign. We want to get rid of them without hurting anyone else. Any ideas?"

Dee raised his hand, "I want a guarantee that there will be no force. Buster and Zelda may be in the Presidential Palace at that time."

Captain O'Spotnid-3 said, "I agree, Mister Dee. Based on the very thin legal justification that Griffer-1 cited for our mission to Earth, I do not like what he stands for. My crew has the courage to do whatever is necessary, and we are committed. But it would make us feel better if we could catch him red-handed committing a crime before we reveal ourselves."

O'Hecknid said, "My colleague and I would derive great pleasure in using our skills on those two marks. Gro Skoo will want to meet with us about our PLUMBOB work on Mother Roost, so it should be a simple matter to frame them up like a stack of two-by-fours. We've lived our whole lives to prepare for such a duping! We can make Griffer and Gro Skoo do whatever you want. A little bribery maybe? I, myself, am a big fan of driving a goon to the point of making death threats. And my mate O'Jecknid here is quite clever at getting himself assaulted for a good cause. Isn't that right, me beauty?"

"You said it!"

Trukk-9 said, "Good, good. And we need them to KNOW that we got their crime on film. So, I propose that we approach this mission as if it were a film production."

"Alright then, Trukk-9, it is fine if you want to use my ship as a filming platform," said Captain O'Spotnid-3. "I have some special help in dispatch. So we won't have any trouble with military reinforcements being called in. I feel safe in saying that this will be a bloodless coup. And as my old friend General O'Buzznid-3 would say, 'Screw them if they cannot tell the truth.' You let me know when you have your shot, and if I am satisfied, I will give the order to decloak."

"Fair enough. How's that for a plan everyone?" asked Kyleence.

"Hey, what about me?!" boomed a very big voice that startled everyone and made Michael and Gregory cry. His hung, but otherwise incomplete avatar appeared. "I am Space Pirate-X and I have a special meteor all ready. I'm going to bounce it off their upper atmosphere right at the perfect moment! You should look for some blue sparks in the tail. It's going to be very impressive! Make sure you get it on film."

Dayv and 'Blood' couldn't handle the strangeness any longer and were now rolling around on the floor honking their beaks off.

Though he may anger you, do not dwell on how to kill the Planet One humanoid by skewering him with your leg spikes, biting his stupid head off, drying out his carcass, and grinding it up for brunch during the high holidays. Oh, sorry…

~ O'Buzznid-3

COUP, THE MOVIE

Trukk-9 sat by himself in the dark. He dangled his legs from the stage of the oldest underground cinema-house on Bukk-9. This was where it had all begun.

He had arrived early. Soon Kyleence and the two sets of twins would arrive. Then Dee with his nieces and nephews, and Stick.E with whichever young sine-wave had taken his fancy lately, would come by to help set up.

It was world premier night. However, this was to be an intimate affair. There would be no klieg lights, no red carpet, and no Dab Tabmow fangirls screaming from the street. His best friends and closest colleagues had succeeded in keeping it a secret. Pure trust.

After Trukk-9's family and two best buddies, Jimmy and Fleence arrived accompanied by Dluhosh and Miles who pushed Mudhosh in front of them on a cart under a portable containment dome. Both Dnooblians displayed their formal black and white skin patterns. Miles had just had his glands cleaned. He ran over to beg popcorn from Buster and Zelda.

Next to arrive, arm in arm, were the Presidential Travelling Secretary and her man, the new Vice President of the Galactic Pool. She scratched his head gently as everyone congratulated them.

Ambassador-nominee Dayv and the rest of the surfer guys and their surfer wives and girlfriends from Mother Roost-19 arrived next.

Then came the former dispatcher widow of Captain O'Spotnid-3, dressed in black and pushing their two surviving grubs in a dual baby carriage. She was followed by the Bee engineer and Ant doctor who had flown in with the Click Beetle pilot. The Moth technicians flew into the theater and looked around to make sure they'd know where the projector light would shine from. 'Dunger' and his old lady rolled into the lot and parked their nest-egg out in the far corner.

O'Hecknid and O'Jecknid arrived next – each wearing a water-squirting corsage.

The only one missing was ULBTX-123, which was no accident.

Once everyone was settled, the footlights came on and Trukk-9 walked out on stage.

"My closest and most trusted friends, welcome to YOUR film. I love you all very much."

The audience cheered and someone from Dee's group shouted, "Trukk-9, you're the man!"

"Aye, but this is not a film about us. This is a film about a galaxy – a new Galactic Pool! And as soon as the attorneys sort things out, it will be a film for all of the people of the Galactic Pool – including our new friends from Mother Roost-19. Welcome aboard!"

The Roostians waved.

"Friends, you will see yourselves in this film. Some of you have, as you know, re-enacted some of your parts. And in some cases I have applied certain stylizations. The result is a more truthful truth. The audience will feel the intensity that you felt. The audience will know the truth that you know. This is not the truth of some bean-counter on Planet One, this is the truth of the soul – an extra truth."

No one understood what that meant, but it sounded good. So they cheered – long and loud.

The curtain opened and the projector lit the screen. The Moths turned around to stare at the projector, but managed to respectfully keep their seats.

The film opens with bombs falling into a jungle, accompanied by a lone Dnooblian tenor and no other sound. There appear to be scattered dwellings in the jungle. The explosions create huge fireballs that almost seem to reach up to the bomber – they look like flaming cauliflowers contrasting violently with the verdant green jungle. This is footage that Trukk-9 stole from an unknown filmmaker on Earth. And it lasts a very long time.

The scene cuts to a training room. There are four uniformed Discreet Service agents sitting on couches twiddling joysticks. Buster and Zelda, played by the real Buster and Zelda, burst into the room.

"We did it! We got a presidential decree for upgrades to our training equipment. Look!" says Buster.

Zelda holds up a set of eleven-framed sunglasses and Buster passes out the rest of the gear to the agents.

Zelda says, "It's a totally interactive full-emersion virtual reality game now. Put on these Dab Tabmow costumes and you'll see what we mean. The tights are equipped with motion sensors. It's really awesome and fun. It will make you into super agents!"

The scene jumps ahead, and now the training room has been cleared of couches and video screens. There are six fully decked-out Dab Tabmows – four big ones and two little ones – jumping and spinning around the room. Each is obviously fighting a battle that only they can see. The soundtrack now plays audio of their enraged enemies and the sounds of blows being landed on bodies.

The scene cuts to a flashing yellow light on the wall and the sound of a claxon. None of the agents notice it.

Then, somewhat confusingly, the film jumps back in time by a half an hour and shows the actual footage that Dee shot of O'Hecknid and O'Jecknid being grabber-beamed down from the cloaked Battleship Aedeagus. The camera follows them out of an alley, then the scene cuts to a split-screen view of the Presidential Palace as seen from the lapel cameras worn by the two Crickets.

The split screen continues to show the process of going through security. The various insectoid guards and screeners wave O'Hecknid and O'Jecknid around the metal detectors, but otherwise do not act as though they recognize the pair.

The next scene is shot through the window into Gro Skoo's office from the cloaked battleship.

"O'Hecknid-3 and O'Jecknid-3, why are you back so soon?" asks Gro Skoo.

"We would like to explain. It is quite an extraordinary story. So extraordinary, in fact, that we think you will want the President here to hear it. Actually, we insist."

"I'm sorry gentlemen, but the President was involved in a terrible fishing accident. He is incapacitated in the hospital. But I think the Vice President will be interested." Gro Skoo calls the office of the Vice President.

Now the scene is through Griffer-1's office window. He is hunched over his desk looking at a video of some kind of mayhem, wringing his hands. His phone rings. The camera zooms into a tight close-up of his lips. Subtitles read what his lips say. "Yeah, bring them over, but make it quick."

Now the Vice President closes the video and shifts into an arrogant pose with his feet up on the desk – the soles of his shoes pointing directly at the door where Gro Skoo and the two Crickets enter. "Okay, make this briefing brief. What did you get?" he asks.

"Sir, we found something interesting. Please have a look at the photos on this memory stick."

Griffer-1 plugs it in and turns on the view screen. Up until then, Griffer-1 has maintained his arrogant desk pose. But the first image makes him sit bolt upright.

"Yes, Mister Vice President, we found a Galactic Class Mountain Melter. And we sure wondered what that might be doing there, didn't we, me old mate?" asks O'Hecknid-3.

"Yep, we sure did! And not only that, but we found the whole crew. And do you know what they told us? They told us that you had sent them to a planet called Dirt."

Now Gro Skoo looks nervous.

Griffer-1 says, "Oh, you must be describing Gro Skoo's little project. Why don't you tell us what that was all about, Gro Skoo?"

"Me? It was never my idea! I was strictly carrying out your orders!"

O'Hecknid says, "Oh, come now, ye old geezers! Don't let's spoil this with a lover's quarrel."

"That's right, fellas. I think we can make this work out fantastically and financially for all of us," says O'Jecknid.

Griffer and Gro Skoo are listening.

"We don't care about some silly battleship! We found something much better. I'm going to place something on your desk, Mister Vice President. You can have it if you like, because I know where there's a lot more of it. If you accept it, however, I will take it to mean that you'd like to do a little deal with us."

The scene changes to the split-screen view from the Crickets' lapel cameras, which each show one side of Griffer-1. O'Hecknid's claw comes into view and places a large gold nugget in front of the Vice President. The nugget is the same weight as a size-eleven golden flip-flop.

Griffer-1 looks up at both Crickets, who have now struck their own arrogant poses.

"Those silly Mother Roostians and that incompetent PLUMBOB team you sent before never realized…" says O'Hecknid. "Now, the whole planet isn't littered with this stuff – just a couple of remote avalanches of it – but we'd be happy to share our coordinates for, say, a mere ten percent of the mining profits each."

The split screen now shows Griffer-1's clawed and furry hand reach out to slip the huge nugget into his desk drawer.

The view now cuts to the bridge of the ship. Captain Spotty says, "There we go! They just admitted their conspiracy and accepted a bribe - and on film too." He gives a nod to Trukk-9 and Dee.

"Audio is nice and clear," says Stick.E.

The scene cuts back to the office. "As an analogy of what I'm trying to say, Mister Vice President, take this vase for example," says O'Jecknid.

"Jolly good!" says O'Hecknid.

O'Jecknid picks up the vase and dumps the little bouquet of catnip and water over the Vice President's balding pate. Then he says, "Whoa, sorry champ! I think there's a towel over there." O'Hecknid points at the window and spins the Vice President's chair so he's facing it.

And the Battleship Aedeagus de-cloaks in full view. Then the view cuts to a tight shot of the passengers and crew standing amongst the foliage on the ship's bridge.

"I see that I have you at a disadvantage, Mister Vice President," says Captain O'Spotnid-3. "Would you perhaps like us to melt something for you? You seem very interested in melting things lately, eh Mister Vice President? We can be very precise. Perhaps we could begin with the little fountain in the Presidential Garden? Or maybe you'd like to begin by having a little chat with an Earthling?"

Dluhosh points at the ship's view screen where a camera is mounted facing back at the crew, and says, "Miles! Kitty cat! Kitty cat! Get the kitty!"

Miles bounds over Dluhosh's control panel toward the screen where he sees what amounts to a large bi-pedal kitty cat in a business suit. He yells, "KILL KILL KILL KILL!"

The view is now a tight close-up of Miles snarling and baring his fangs. The camera's fish-eye lens makes Miles appear huge compared to the background. Gregory's voice shouts from Miles' mouth. "That's it sucker! We have had enough of you! The Earthlings who came before must not have been scary enough for you, so now I've taken over this battleship and its crew. And I intend to complete the mission this time. I am called Snarlbeast! At my command, this captain will launch me into your office. Mere melting isn't good enough! I eat twerps like you, and then I puke them up and eat them again, you little kitty cat!"

At the sound of 'kitty cat' Miles yells KILL KILL KILL again.

A meteoric blood-red fireball streaks across the sky trailing blue sparkles. Miles bounds back into Dluhosh's lap and gets a nice piece of bacon.

Griffer-1 pushes the emergency Discrete Service button on his desk again and again, but no agents come to his rescue. He picks up his desk microphone and screams. "Dispatch! Get the military to my office! I need a humanoid crew on a fully-armed battleship right now!"

A small voice comes over the radio. "Is this the Vice President calling?"

"YES!"

"Oh, I'm sorry. Do you have the President's approval?"

"Get them here now! There's a mutiny in progress!"

"I will be happy to sir, as soon as I get the order from the President. Please call me back when you have his permission – I'll be here."

The view on the movie screen zooms to Griffer-1's trembling and sweaty face until the image blurs into stylized fever-dream hallucinations. The outraged and frightened Vice President's vision of the crew aboard the battleship becomes distorted and wiggly around the edges, and tracers follow everything that moves. Individual faces emerge from a forest, warping and ballooning to fill Griffer-1's mind. A beautiful Conversation Hostess taunts him for having tiny feet. Big ugly birds honk derisively at him. Dnooblians snap their tentacles, and the Vice President hallucinates his own entrails spilling out. He sees a lifetime's worth of mice come back to life and chew their way out of his intestines. A Dung Beetle hurls its lunch at him. Two beautiful little babies wearing tiny sailor outfits twirl in mid-air like pinwheels, making rude gestures at him and screaming "Intercourse with you, female canine!"

The vision of little babies with normal feet screaming such vile and unnecessary language brings Griffer-1 back to reality. He slaps at the Discreet Service call button some more.

The view switches back to the bridge of the battleship. Trukk-9 is pointing at something in the Vice President's office. Dee turns the camera toward it. Trukk-9 yells, "What in holy hell is that?!"

Griffer-1 now looks up to see his Vice Presidential Cricket coming at him with some kind of nozzled contraption. Griffer-1 sees the compound menace in the Cricket's eyes. He dives on top of his desk and pulls open a hidden panel. He flips a pair of switches, and a red light comes on. Then he pushes a code into a keypad. He looks up expectantly just as he's hit in the face by a very cold blast of decompressed calming agent fog. Griffer-1 flips the switches and punches in the code again. He looks up, but whatever he expects to happen, doesn't happen.

The Vice Presidential Cricket continues to blast the Vice President – holding the nozzle at point blank range, forcing the vapor right up his little nose.

The view cuts back to another stylized Vice Presidential hallucination. This time it's a single red rose petal drifting down to the ground in slow motion. It drifts and falls, drifts and falls, seemingly on an endless descent.

The Vice Presidential Cricket doesn't take time to fully assess the situation before he runs for the door to the Discreet Service office. He opens it and finally gets their attention. Six Dab Tabmows charge into the Vice President's office, spinning and kicking. The four bigger Dab Tabmows remove their gaming hoods and immediately go for O'Hecknid and O'Jecknid, but the view cuts to Fleence who says, "Nice outfits boys. I like the way your tights emphasize your best features."

The four Discrete Service agents fall to the floor, twitching in ecstasy, temporarily disabled.

Captain O'Spotnid-3 calls out. "Mister Vice Presidential Cricket! Please listen! We have evidence of great crimes committed by these two. Please hear us out."

The Vice Presidential Cricket looks out the window and says, "I'm listening."

Trukk-9 explains.

Griffer-1 stirs and is hit by another blast of calming agent. The rose petal continues to drift, ever downward.

Trukk-9 says, "I think you need to declare the Vice President incapacitated so that you can begin the process of fixing the damage."

"But I cannot make such a declaration, as I am the successor," explains the Vice Presidential Cricket.

"Really?" says Trukk-9.

"It would be a conflict of interest, Mister Trukk-9. Only the President or the Sublime Court can make that declaration." He hits Griffer-1 with another blast of calming agent.

The littlest Dab Tabmow steps up and says, "I'm a Presidential Commissioner, so I think I have the authority of the President, right?" Zelda removes her gaming glasses and hood.

The four Discreet Service agents agree with her. The group captain says, "She's right, you know. Her words become law. There is no other explanation."

Zelda says, "The angry man should be taken away before he hurts himself. He shouldn't be allowed to do anything where he could get hurt."

"He could accidentally stab himself with a pen while he is signing a document, perhaps?" asks the Vice Presidential Cricket. "Is that what you mean?"

"Yeah, buddy. The way he gets all excited, you bet he could. He could put his eye out!" says Zelda.

The group captain asks, "So, Zelda, you are saying that he should be declared incapacitated?"

"No, you shouldn't capacitate him. That's a little bit too severe, isn't it? Just tell him he isn't allowed to do anything until he gets better."

The Discrete Service officers take the 'angry old man' and the canister of calming agent and start toward the door. Gro Skoo comes out from under the desk and files in with Griffer-1 as the agents led them away.

Buster is still spinning and kicking in the far corner of the office, oblivious as he works toward an all-time high score on the *Dab Tabmow, ManCricket* video game.

O'Hecknid and O'Jecknid retrieve the gold, and then high-two each other.

And the film ends with a montage of Zelda-15 carrying out various presidential duties to the strains of Mother Roostian campfire banjo picking.

***

The curtain closed and the theater erupted in applause.

As the applause died down, a small voice at the back of the theater spoke. It was Zelda. "But I don't want to be President of the Galactic Pool anymore. I have too much schoolwork."

Then Dluhosh said, "Don't worry honey, Mudhosh and I have a plan…"

Do not believe what the humanoid says about the Dnooblian.
They are just bitter about being eviscerated.
~ O'Buzznid-3

PRESIDENTIAL MEMORY

In a heavily guarded room deep within the main hospital on Planet One, the senior nurse approached the President's bedside. She was fierce-looking in her tiger-striped fur with gray highlights around her muzzle. "Sir, we are going to remove your calming agent drip. Do you understand?"

"Prrrrr… yeaaaah. No… yeah… whaaaa huhnnn?" asked the President.

"Sir, we are going to test to see if you have improved. We have to see whether you are able to carry on with your duties. You were in quite a state when you first came in, sir. And we cannot wipe your memory until there is a ruling from the Sublime Court, and they are not scheduled to hear the appeal for several weeks, sir. It's even possible that they may rule AGAINST any presidential memory wipe. So you have to try very hard on your own. Are you ready?"

"W-w-whoa…" said the President.

The nurse pulled the drip of full-strength liquid calming agent. She and the grabber beam tech, along with a roomful of Discrete Service agents and legal advisors, waited.

The President raised his hand to wipe the drool from the fur around his mouth. His eyes opened a little wider. He rolled his head to the side and looked around the room at all the people looking back at him. His lips moved as if to form a word. "I'm a… man… of the people…" he slurred.

"Sir, can you hear me?"

"Nurrrrssssh… Hi… there. Ummm…"

"That's good, Mister President. Now please try to answer the questions that this nice team of attorneys is going to ask you. Okay, sir?"

"Okaaaay…"

The first attorney spoke. "Mister President. Can you tell us who you are?"

"I, I, I… man of… people…"

"Very good, sir. Now can you tell us your name?

"Mommmmy… It's… it's little Gren-Gren Wee-Wee… Maaaa…"

"He seems normal to me," said one of the other attorneys. About half of the remaining attorneys nodded in agreement.

"No, this is not normal," said the nurse. "Please continue, but I don't want to hear any extraneous legal talk out of you until I say he's normal. You understand?"

"Yes ma'am," said the lead attorney as he shot the evil-eye at the other attorney. "Sir, do you know where you are?"

"Fish… Fishin' with J-J-Jimmy…"

"Give him a few more moments," said the nurse.

The President's eyes opened wide, his claws sprung, his marzipan-like musk issued forth, and he screamed, "EEEEEEEEEEEEEEEEEEEEEEEEEEEELLLLLLLL!

GHAAAA! EEL EEL EEL EEL!" He sprung straight up and sunk his claws into the padded ceiling and continued screaming 'eel' while hanging from above.

The grabber beam tech encased him, and the nurse pushed the calming agent button and held it in. The tech lowered the President back into his bed, and the nurse re-administered the drip.

"Everyone out!" she said. And the attorneys did not argue with her.

The nurse and the attorneys tested the President once a week, and got the same basic result each time. Meanwhile, the appeal to the Sublime Court dragged on and on.

***

Dluhosh and Mudhosh hovered in their cloaked ship a few hundred feet up, and within visual range of the hospital.

Dluhosh said, "Mudhosh, I have to ask you something. This isn't rogue to rogue – this is Dnooblian to Dnooblian."

"Sure, Dluhosh."

"Are you willing to kill for this mission?"

"No. But I am willing to die."

"Really? Die?" said Dluhosh.

"Oh Dluhosh, I don't know – I don't even understand why we are here. I lost track when the Vice President saw the rude swirly babies in Trukk-9's movie. What ARE we doing, Dluhosh?"

"Okay, I've rigged my memory wiper to be more-or-less portable. We are going to get into the hospital. I'm going to take the memory wiper to within range of the President's hospital room. We are going to selectively wipe his memory of the eel attack. And maybe one other thing that he seems to be suppressing."

"That sounds pretty risky. But what am I supposed to do?" asked Mudhosh.

"Yes, it's very risky, so what you are supposed to do is very important. If I get caught even being in possession of a PLUMBOB memory wiper, I'm going to prison. And if we are caught using it on the President, well, you get it right? You want rogue-appropriate behavior? Here you go."

"Yes, but what am I supposed to do, Dluhosh?"

"You will carry the power source and hard drive. You also need to man the wire that connects to my wiper unit, and keep a look out."

"How are we going to get in and out? My camo skills aren't as good as yours, Dluhosh. And Dnooblians kind of create panic, don't we?"

"Yep, and that's why the plan will work. Ever ride in a wheelchair, Mudhosh…?"

***

"Dnooblians coming through! Dnooblians coming through!" shouted Dluhosh as he wheeled Mudhosh into the hospital at full sprint. "Injured Dnooblian coming through! Clear the corridor!"

At this, all the humanoids and everyone else who knew what was good for them got out of the way. Dluhosh ran up the main hall until he found an open room. He ducked in and locked the door behind them.

"Okay, I'm going into the ventilation system. You feed me this wire and I'll explore until I'm able to tune in his brain. It may be a pretty weak signal. If there's trouble out here, jerk the wire a few times. If worse comes to worse and they get through the door, remember to shout 'Injured Dnooblian, clear the way!' Okay?"

Dluhosh oozed his way through the maze of ventilation shafts. Each time he turned a corner he checked the readings on his handheld unit. He was looking for a mind that had a high-magnitude band of terror in the correct place. He was examining a candidate when the wire jerked several times. He backtracked on the wire as fast as his tentacles could pull him through the shafts. Back at the room he asked through the grated vent, "What's up!?"

Mudhosh replied, "Huh?"

"You yanked the wire."

"Oh, sorry, I was probably just laughing. I thought of something that Trukk-9 could have put in the movie – something really obvious that he missed. I'll have to tell him about it."

Dluhosh crawled back through the ducts. He zeroed back in on the candidate brain. It showed a big terror spike at about the time of the eel attack. It could definitely be the President. But to verify this, he scanned the mind back in time looking for the trauma from when Gregory, Michael, and Jimmy had attacked him in his office. He scanned back and forth a couple of times in the right time zone before he noticed the time counter jump forward by several minutes. He scanned back again. Sure enough, there was an eighteen-and-a-half-minute gap in the correct spot. Someone else had apparently extracted that memory from the President's brain.

The wire yanked again. Dluhosh tried to rush through the President's brain's timeline back to the memory of the eel attack. But he went too fast and ended up all the way around the loop to the President's earliest memories. The red trauma spikes popped up in increasing frequency before Dluhosh could reverse. The wire tugged again. Dluhosh had no choice but to press alt-F5, which erased every traumatic memory from the President's entire life.

Gone was the severe beating by the elderly lady with the precision cane. Gone was getting his ear caught in the automatic envelope licker in Gro Skoo's office. No more wedgies, no more catnip in his porridge, and no more being afraid of mice.

"What's up!?" whispered Dluhosh through the vent for a second time.

"Huh?"

"The wire!"

"Oh, sorry, I was practicing my camo. Watch this. I can make myself look like that biohazard container."

"Mudhosh, let's go!"

Mudhosh got back in the wheelchair and Dluhosh pushed yelling, "Dnooblians coming through!"

When they made it back to Dluhosh's ship, he said, "It'll be interesting to see who wakes up when the President regains consciousness."

The dreams of the Cricket, the dreams of the Moth, the dreams of the Ant; these are no less important than the dreams of Planet One.
~ O'Buzznid-3

BUG ZAPPER

Griffer-1 and Gro Skoo sat in the cockpit of Gro Skoo's personal flying saucer. Griffer hadn't resorted to leading him there at gunpoint, but he was prepared to just in case.

Gro Skoo had taken a plea deal and retired from his position in the Presidential Palace. He was happy in retirement.

Griffer-1 had fought the charges and lost. But for some reason, the Sublime Court let him off with community service, which he had failed to perform.

"I'm not taking off until you tell me where we are going, Griffer," said Gro Skoo.

Griffer grimaced and hissed from the side of his mouth.

"Okay, but I'm not stopping the ship until you tell me where we are and why we're there." Gro Skoo lifted the ship off.

"How good are you with your grabber beam?" asked Griffer-1.

"Oh, you know, I'm getting there. I guess I'm as good as I am with my riding lawnmower. You saw my lawn."

"Yes, I did, but you better not screw this up."

"Screw WHAT up?" asked Gro Skoo.

"You remember in my office when those kung fu Crickets came spinning in?"

"Yeah…"

"Remember how I dove onto my desk and opened that hidden panel?"

"Right, I was expecting a trap door to open under those horrible Crickets," said Gro Skoo.

"That's right. The big trap door… That's where we're going. Just head to these coordinates. You'll see it when we get there."

"Come on, Griffer. You have to tell me more."

"I flipped the toggles in the correct order and I pushed the right code in. I know I did. But nothing happened. They should all be dead. All of them…"

"I don't like the sound of this, Griffer."

Griffer-1reached under his coat and pulled out his ray blaster. He pointed it at Gro Skoo.

"Fly."

Gro Skoo flew. After a few minutes he said, in a very calm and reassuring tone, "So do you miss the power, Griffer? It sure was neat having all that power. We could make people do exactly what was good for them. We sure helped a lot of the right people, didn't we? We sure were a good team. But, you know, that was A LOT of responsibility. All the law suits and scandals and everything all the time… No, I don't miss that. It's refreshing to wake up in the morning and not be worried about covering our asses on some silly thing or another. Don't you agree, Griffer?"

"They were getting uppity. Couldn't you sense it?"

"Who?"

"The bugs. Always turning up where you didn't expect them. Making eye contact. Speaking directly at me. Gnashing their jaws. Using contractions... Gro Skoo, they have to be stopped."

"Yes, I noticed some changes in the insectoids' attitudes. But I never really understood why they had to be that subservient in the first place," said Gro Skoo.

"Because of THIS, you idiot!" said Griffer-1. "They've taken over!"

"Okay, okay, I get it. Take it easy..."

"I will not take it easy. I intend to put things right and reclaim what is mine. It should have worked. We tested it extensively. It even worked in the vacuum of space. It would have covered light years... What the hell went wrong? They all should have... They all should have zapped over dead..."

"Who? The insectoids? What do you mean?" asked Gro Skoo.

"The Bug and Arthropod Rectification Project – BAARP. It was Rim Ram-1's idea. Only he and I knew. We had Crickets build it. They thought it was a second generation galactic autotranslator. It was almost sad to see how proud of it they were." Griffer smiled that crooked smile of his.

***

They reached the tower and Griffer said, "Okay, Skoo, put her in auto-hover right next to the dome on top. The device is inside. I've deactivated the force field. I want you to fix a grabber beam around my chest. I'm going out."

"Going out!? Are you nuts?"

Griffer pointed his blaster at Gro Skoo again.

"And tie me off to something with this line around my waist in case you screw up with the grabber beam."

"Griffer, Griffer, this is crazy! We aren't construction workers, Griffer. What are you going to do with that screwdriver? I'm not that good with the grabber beam!"

"Shut up! Open the hatch!"

Gro Skoo opened the hatch right next to the device on top of the tower. The air from outside hit them with a rancid blast that made their eyes sting and almost gave them whiplash.

"AHHHHGGGH! What is that smell!?" asked Gro Skoo. "Phooeeee!"

"I think we found the problem! That nasty stuff has probably seeped in." Griffer-1 leaned out to have a closer look. "Yep, it dissolved the main seal. I'm going to have to open the housing!"

Griffer clamped his screwdriver between his teeth, tucked away his blaster, and made the short leap to a crossbeam on the tower's lattice just below the bug zapper. He tried to grab the bar, but a healthy coating of churdle lard caused him to lose his grip.

Gro Skoo – not being a construction worker – had tied Griffer-1's back-up safety line to the post of his chair right above where the wheels attach. Griffer-1's weight pulled Gro Skoo away from the grabber beam controls and right out the port.

They fell about three-hundred feet before hitting the packing peanuts. Everything went black around them, and their fall slowed as Gro Skoo's robe filled with peanuts and acted as a drogue. They struggled – sinking little by little through the darkness. They eventually ended up face-to-face with Gro Skoo on top.

"Get off of me and stop your whimpering, Skoo!"

"I can't move! I think I'm wrapped in the safety line! Can't you cut it?!"

Griffer dug out his blaster and fired it blindly. It didn't hit anything, but it did succeed in melting a few feet of packing peanuts around them. They were now bound nose-to-nose inside a cocoon.

***

Ships passing within range had been picking up the ping of a craft on auto-hover for a couple of months. A terraforming service ship that was returning to Planet One from ZZZZZZ-3 ahead of schedule requested clearance to investigate.

The pilot called the dispatcher and said, "The ping is coming from a private vessel at the top of a mountain. It's coming into visual range. Huh, there appears to be a high tower – black and with no signal light on top – very strange. And, yeah, there's a small vessel hovering with its port open."

By now, the biodegradable packing peanuts had melted in the rain, turned to dust, and blown off to be incorporated into the topsoil.

"Wait, I see something at the base of the tower. It looks like a big wad of mauve fabric. Must be a parachute… Dispatcher, I think we're going to need the coroner."

The pilot landed the ship and a Moth technician flew out to investigate. He looked under Gro Skoo's robe. "Hey! There are two victims, and one of them is still alive!"

Griffer-1 was still hanging on, but just barely. He was wedged between two jagged rocks – emaciated, hypothermic, dehydrated and gangrenous. But his old heart just kept whirring along.

The Moth cut the safety line from Gro Skoo's chair, and the pilot pulled Griffer-1 into the ship with a grabber beam.

"What about the other victim?" yelled the pilot.

The Moth replied. "There's nothing left of him but well-gnawed bones!"

It is not just the insectoid who starts life as a grub. Some humanoids also start life as grubs and then metamorphose to be almost as beautiful as Moths.
~ O'Buzznid-3

A NEW PRESIDENT

"Good morning Mister President. How are we feeling today?" asked the Praying Mantis assistant nurse.

"I feel great! Never better, in fact. You folks sure do a wonderful job here. That Cricket fella who was in here tidying up earlier – I didn't get his name, but he was a very interesting man. He told me about his hero, the former Vice Presidential Cricket – said his name was General O'Buzznid-3. I must have met him on numerous occasions, but I don't really recall. Anyway, he gave me a copy of O'Buzznid-3's memoir. It's very interesting. I had no idea that all these terrible things had happened to your people. They never taught us this stuff in history class."

"Yes, sir, we've had a difficult past, but lately things have been looking up. Thanks to you…"

"Thanks to me? What have I done? All I've done lately is to be a useless and annoying fishing partner to my friend Jimmy."

"Sir, you signed some very progressive decrees into law during the weeks leading up to your accident. Your support among insectoids has skyrocketed. They say you are a cinch to win the next election," said the assistant nurse.

"Wow! I bet Griffer will finally be proud of me. But somehow it doesn't matter anymore…"

"Yes, Mister President, there is a lot for you to catch up on. As soon as you are well enough, the head nurse said you could have visitors. Do you think you are ready to see someone who can answer a lot of questions for you?"

"Sure! I'd enjoy the company. Bring them in anytime."

The nurse left and the President went back to reading *I, Buzzy*. He uttered the occasional tut-tut and jotted notes in the margins.

Then a pair of Crickets came into the room.

"Howdy!" said the President from his bed. He held out his hand to shake their tarsi. He realized that he'd never done this with an insectoid before, and wondered why he hadn't.

"Hello, Mister President. My name is O'Smegnid-3, but you can call me Smeggy if you have trouble with insectoid names. I am the former Vice Presidential Cricket."

"Oh, just like General O'Buzznid-3 – he was the Vice Presidential Cricket too! Glad to know ya!" said the President.

"Yes, I have some very large boots to fill, as it were. And this is Zelda-15. We are very pleased to see that you have regained your health and spirit."

"Yeah, because I'm tired of being president," said Zelda. "It sure is a lot of work. I'm falling behind in my classes and I might even have to go to summer school!"

"Well, young lady, you should definitely keep up with your schooling. I'm sure you have a bright future. But, uh, I don't understand. Tired of being PRESIDENT…?" said the President.

Vice President Smeggy explained. Then he said, "Mister President, it seems that former Vice President Griffer-1 had an even more serious accident than yours, and he has had to take an early retirement. And thanks to a decree that you signed shortly before your accident, I am now your new Vice President."

"Oh yes… I remember… Gosh, without that decree I'd be talking to that smelly Fermamentian from the Galactic Assembly right now, huh? My Presidential Travelling Secretary is the best! I owe her a big thanks for that one. How is she doing, by the way?"

"Mister President, I like to think she's happy. Peggy is my wife now," said Smeggy.

"Congratulations! Heh heh, just don't let her get into your head too soon!"

"Well stated, Mister President. I shall endeavor to keep the itch at bay until the end of your second term."

"I'd appreciate that. Now, when can you get me out of this hospital? I have a lot of work to do."

"Yes, sir. The Discreet Service will take you to the Presidential Palace as soon as you are ready."

The President signaled for his new Vice President to come closer and then whispered something into his tympanum.

"Yes, certainly sir!" said Smeggy.

***

A few hours later, the presidential motorcade arrived at the Presidential Palace. There was a huge crowd of palace staff and their families assembled on the front grounds. They were all there, many of them carrying heart-felt messages on signs they held up over their heads. They cheered when the President stepped out of his limo saucer.

The entire Galactic Assembly was there, with the exception of a certain Fermamentian Viscount. The Squirrel representatives from Cache-6 chattered their welcome from the tops of the trees. The Bearmen and Bearwomen of Free-15 hooted a chant from their huddle in the middle of everything. The Crab People of Flat Rock-13 snapped their claws together from under their portable flat rocks. The Dnooblian delegation flashed colors of welcome and respect. And an enormous Swamp Master of perhaps forty-feet in height stood politely off to the side clapping.

The President looked upon the crowd made up of the all the various peoples of his Galactic Pool, including a delegation of large avianoids that he did not recognize. He wiped a tear from his eye, and said, "I'm overwhelmed, thank you all. I'm not sure what I've done to deserve this, because, well, I have to admit to being a bit of a lazy bastard during my first term. I promise to do a much better job in the future if I'm re-elected. Now, my new Vice President has been briefing me, and I plan to make the ribbon cutting for the newly restored ZZZZZZ-3 one of my top priorities. For I am a man of all the people!"

The crowd went crazy. Many insectoids rose in spontaneous flight and circled the President while singing all of their songs simultaneously.

A Discreet Service group captain said, "And Mister President, this gentleman is the Ambassador from the newest planet in the Galactic Pool. This is Ambassador Dayv-19 and his flock from Mother Roost-19. They won by a landslide in the recent vote for acceptance. Congratulations, sir."

"Welcome to the Galactic Pool my friends!" said the President.

"You bet, daddy-o! We are thrilled to represent!" said Ambassador Dayv.

"What wonderful news!" said the President. "You know what Rim Ram-1used to say – 'New planets make the Galaxy shine brighter.' Actually, that's kind of a stupid thing to say when you think about it…"

***

The President entered his office.

"SURPRISE!"

His new inner-circle gathered themselves around the President's desk. The Presidential Travelling Secretary presented the President with a small flowering plant that used to be native on ZZZZZZ-3 – and would hopefully be common there again.

The Vice President released a mouse. And when that little game had ended, the President's new part-time student-advisor, Zelda, rolled a large parchment out on the desk.

"Here's the decree you asked for, Prez. I even proof-read it! Miss Peggy the Travelling Secretary helped me with the spelling too."

"Thank you, Miss Zelda." The President read the decree. "This looks great! I think I'm ready to sign it, but please tell me – who is that and what is he doing?"

They all looked over at a little Dab Tabmow in the corner who was performing a series of three-sixty power kicks.

"Oh, that's my brother, Buster. His full name is O'Buzznid-3 Junior Buster-15."

"Wow, that's quite a mouthful. Did you say O'Buzznid-3 Junior?"

"Yep! Our daddy was General O'Buzznid-3."

"You mean THE General O'Buzznid-3?"

"Yeah buddy!"

"Well then I think it would be appropriate for your brother to sign this decree alongside my signature. What do you think about that, Zelda?"

"That would be cool!"

"Great! But what is he doing right now? Can we interrupt him?" asked the President.

"He's probably going for a new high score, so we should wait," replied Zelda.

Everyone watched with amusement as Buster twisted into a final Multi-Vision Tornado Attack (Level 11). When he landed, he pulled his gaming hood off and said, "Yeah! New high score!"

Everyone applauded.

"I recorded it too, so you can see the whole thing once I upload it. Uh, so what's going on?"

In a very good approximation of the correct Cricketish pronunciation, the President said, "Mister O'Buzznid-3 Junior Buster-15, I would like to ask you to co-sign this decree with me."

"Sure. What's it for, buddy?"

"This decree abolishes the Treaty of Do What We Say. It restores full citizenship rights to all insectoids, and there is a provision that requires the Galactic Broadcasting Company trust fund to provide back-pay and reparations to all insectoids who have served the Galactic Pool."

"Hey, that sounds pretty cool!" said Buster. "But why me? Because of my high score?"

"No, though that is very impressive, Mister O'Buzznid-3 Junior. It is because I want the name O'Buzznid-3 forever etched in history for something good. Your daddy would be proud."

***

On Chuffed-18, the gang watched the live TV feed of the President's arrival at the Presidential Palace.

"Gosh, he seems like a fella I wouldn't mind going fishing with now," said Jimmy.

When it was over, Kyleence spoke up. "Okay everybody, Trukk-9 and I would like to make a little announcement, so listen up. In thanks for all they've done, we have a couple of things that we'd like to present to Dluhosh and Mudhosh. First, Dluhosh, if you'll turn and look out the window…"

Dluhosh turned and saw it decloak. He turned a very deep blue, for he understood. It was a replica of the Cruiser Duke Sukk-9. The only differences were its paintjob – an iridescent, swirly mother-of-pearl pattern, which was the correct and accurate color of Dnooblian high determination – and the large red ribbon tied around it. Dluhosh was speechless.

And before Dluhosh could come up with the words, Trukk-9 made the other presentation. "And Mudhosh, I've reviewed your paintings and outrageous science fiction stories, and I've arranged for you to have your own animated series on my channel. I'll be working with you and your top-notch team to produce whatever your artistic sensibilities tell you to create. And we've developed this mobile containment dome emitter that clips onto your thong. That way you'll be able to go anywhere you like without… You know..."

"Yay!" said Mudhosh.

Dluhosh said, "Trukk-9, I don't know what to say…"

"Don't worry about it Dluhosh. I finally got us those quantum radios I've always wanted. So when you think of what to say, you can call me from anywhere in the galaxy and say it! Plus, we've set it up so you can attach your little PLUMBOB vessel to it like a dinghy. What do you think you'll want to christen it?"

"That's easy," said Dluhosh. "She will be called Cruiser Djenimboo-10 after my special lady back on Dnooblia."

Dee began sobbing, but tried, again, to make it sound like he was coughing. But he was betrayed by the galactic autotranslator. He waved his finger in the wrong direction and said, "HA! I got you, sucker!"

As odd as it may seem to non-Crickets, once the itch begins, it suddenly makes perfect sense to have your head devoured by your special lady.
~ O'Buzznid-3

BOUNTY-2

Dluhosh and Miles paid a visit to Fleence. The visit was ostensibly a reason to get together for a little friendly reunion and let the babies play with their little doggie. But Dluhosh had something bigger in mind that he wanted to discuss.

They relived some old times, got caught up on news, and enjoyed some Earth cuisine (anchovies).

"So Fleence, the main thing I want to talk to you about is this. There's something I'd like to do for you. Um, I'd like to try to find Bounty-2 for you," said Dluhosh.

"Really?! How are you going to do that? It's been expunged from the records. We even asked Zelda to check the insectoid library. There's nothing."

"The way I figure it, if ULBTX-123 made multiple trips between Bounty and Earth, then there would be a line of wormholes at various points between them. One of these wormholes must have been close to Planet One for them to have gotten to it with their technology. If they then encountered a wormhole freeway, Bounty may be farther away than anyone expected, BUT it will be on a line extending from Earth through Planet One. We'd just need to continue that line until we ran out of wormholes."

"Okay…" said Fleence. "But ULBTX-123 caught them and would have destroyed the wormholes, right?"

"He hates scrubbing space, and he's pretty lazy. So I'd bet he only scrubbed the one closest to Planet One. By connecting the dots and checking for another wormhole farther down the line, I'd have a pretty high confidence of being able to find Bounty by continuing. Then the question becomes: What to do?"

"Oh, I think I know what to do… Yes, there are probably moral considerations – I know. But our population is stolen from them, and they are stolen from Earth. So to me it seems like any morality is already broken, and possibly needs to be fixed. At some point it all comes down to sex anyway," said Fleence.

"I understand. But a lot depends on what we find there, don't you think?" asked Dluhosh.

"Sure, like maybe they went extinct."

"Yes, that would make the answer much simpler. But if they are still in a stone-age culture, or if they have advanced to a state like Earth... Does that make a difference?" asked Dluhosh.

"If they ended up anything like Earth, then I think it might be too dangerous – otherwise I'd be begging you to abduct more Earthling guys. But if it's still like the olden days, then maybe it would safe," said Fleence.

"Let me propose something to you," said Dluhosh. "I'll go see if I can find the next wormhole and return with the results. Then we can talk about what to do next. Hopefully it will only take a few months."

"Um, so how much room do you have on your new ship? Like how many girls could you actually take there on a conjugal visit if it came down to that?" asked Fleence.

"If they don't mind sharing berths, I can probably accommodate twenty."

"Oh, they won't mind. But the way I see it, you should take them with you on the exploratory voyage. You never know…"

"That would make it more efficient for me – if they don't mind ending up disappointed."

Miles jumped up on Fleence's lap. He said, "It would make a great TV show. I'd watch it."

"That may be, Miles, but the Bountyans may not understand what it means to sign a model release. So their consent may not be legit," said Dluhosh.

"I for one do not care about television shows," said Fleence. "I just care about increasing our genetic diversity."

"How would you select the passengers?"

"I could start by calling the girls on Jacques' to-do list," said Fleence. "I'm sure they can find the time…"

***

"Alright ladies, this could be it," said Dluhosh.

All twenty descendants of Bountyan clone slaves turned their attention to the view screen.

"I suggest we fly cloaked into the atmosphere and survey for technology. If it seems safe, we can see if there are any men to abduct."

So Dluhosh flew the Cruiser Djenimboo-10 into the planet's atmosphere. A quick sampling of the air suggested no advanced technology. There were also no obvious population centers.

"In this case, a good place to look would be near the mouths of major rivers," said Dluhosh.

So they flew to a likely-looking one at mid-latitude. They located smoke, which led them to a small settlement. "Humanoids! Do they look right to you?"

The eldest of the Chuffed-18 women said, "Oh my… They are so… Look at them! Yes, Dluhosh. Even if they aren't the Bountyans, they'd do nicely. Oh… Just look at that one's butt! I've never seen anything like it. It's so… I don't know… Yummy?"

"Oh yes! Yes! It's so… Rawr!" said one of the women. Some of the women giggled nervously, and the rest were dumbstruck.

They waited until they saw a group of men heading out to hunt and/or gather. The men had heavy beards and matted locks. They carried spears and were dressed in furs.

The men freaked out, but not any worse than any other sapient species when being abducted for the first time. And Dluhosh, believing that these former Earthlings would have a high tolerance for calming agent, triple-dosed them.

However, these guys had a mythology that included the legends of the Planet One raids from so long ago. So they were more angry than surprised or frightened at encountering the aliens. They tried to jab at Dluhosh and Miles with their spears. Dluhosh hit them with more calming agent – pushing the boundaries of what might produce a lethal calm in an Earthling. Finally they sat down and looked around at stuff.

Dluhosh said, "Hello. We are on an unofficial mission. Our only rule is that we will try to be democratic. Your memories of this will be wiped, but that should not stop you from enjoying the benefits of our visit."

"We know who you are. You are Hyena. You are the one who stole the hot women of an entire generation. Our population has never fully recovered our former beauty. And as soon as I can get my anger back up, I'm going to kill you," said the eldest man.

"Ah, yes, I see what you mean. There is, however, another possibility related to that Hyena problem of yours…"

The contingent of women from Chuffed-18 stepped out of the elevator.

"We have come back," said the eldest woman.

The group of men got on their knees and bowed to the women.

"Oh don't be silly. We are women and we need some men, that is all."

"But you are the Daughters of the Stolen Ones. What else do you need? We will house you and care for you – whatever you need – feed you meat every day!"

A couple of the ladies giggled at this offer.

"We would give our lives, Daughters of the Stolen Ones."

Dluhosh said, "I'm afraid that this is not an option. It is against the law for us to be here, and the women cannot stay."

"What do you need? Anything."

"Well, to be blunt, we need to have sex with you. Several times, probably – or at least until the scan shows zygote formation in each of us. In exchange, we will cure you of any diseases or nagging injuries. Then we will send you back after wiping your memories. Deal?"

"Daughters of the Stolen Ones, we would die for you if you asked. So, yes, it's a deal."

The other guys nodded in agreement and one of them said, "Praise be unto the Daughters of the Stolen Ones!"

Dluhosh activated the probaluator. One of the men stabbed at it with his spear, but the eldest man explained that it was most likely okay. They felt much better and fitter in an instant. The Daughters of the Stolen Ones showed the men to their accommodations.

***

"Dluhosh, it's been two weeks. Come on. Let's go do something fun, man. They must be pregnant by now," said Miles.

"Guys, they won't let me see the scans. I just have to take their word for it."

"Look, it only takes a few seconds for an Earthling to get pregnant. Two weeks is ridiculous. And that music they're playing is driving me nuts, you know."

"Only seconds? Okay, now it makes sense that you could survive all those erotic memories you are carrying. Alright then – I'll call time on them." Dluhosh got on the intercom and said, "Ladies and gentlemen, our allotted time on this planet has expired. Please prepare for disembarkation."

A few minutes later, five clean-shaven men dressed in furs and carrying spears stepped out of the elevator and onto the bridge. Dluhosh reprobaluated them in case they had suffered any injuries during the ritual, or had picked up any viruses from the ladies. He wiped their memories as he placed them back on the ground.

After they had scattered, Miles said, "Hey, I don't remember there being a little short one. They look a lot different being clean shaven, but none were that short. I'm sure of it."

Dluhosh got back on the intercom. "Um, ladies, there seems to be an extra man. We did not welcome a little short guy onboard. Where did he come from?"

A minute later, a taller man stepped off the elevator. Once he had been processed, Dluhosh asked, "Ladies, please all come to the bridge before we depart."

When all twenty of them had arrived, Dluhosh asked, "Is it necessary for me to scan the ship for life signs?"

They talked amongst themselves before two of them left. In a minute one of them returned with seven more guys.

Dluhosh processed and dumped them. "It looks like I need to scan the ship. I'm disappointed. I guess it's my fault for not locking the grabber beams at night."

The second woman returned with four more guys wearing disheveled furs. Miles noticed something odd – a piece of fabric that seemed out of place. "Um, Dluhosh, man, you might want to take a peak under the furs." he said.

Dluhosh ordered them to remove the furs. Two guys wore matching white bikini bottoms, each bearing a single golden tassel. Another man had on a black churdle-leather studded jock strap. And the fourth man wore only a handful of creatively glued-on rhinestones. All four men bore signs of bikini waxing.

One of the men said, "Please, sir, allow us to remain here with the Daughters of the Stolen Ones. We are in love with them, sir."

Miles said, "No can do, Mister Caveman."

Dluhosh dumped them and ran the life-sign scan. It turned up twenty more guys. Most of them wore or bore some sign of cosmetic enhancement, including various tattoos and unusual haircuts. "These guys are going to have a lot of trouble explaining themselves."

Miles said, "Their mythology is about to get a lot more interesting."

"Trying to save a man each, I see. Sorry ladies – but, um, I guess the flasks of seed are okay to take." Dluhosh processed the men back to the surface and then readied for departure.

But he never thought to scan the dinghy – where all the best-looking men were stowed away.

I was awarded the Chitin Cross for exceptional resistance to insectoidicide. But there was no red carpet for me.
~ O'Buzznid-3

AWARDS

"The envelope, please! And the winner is… Sally Lightfoot-13 for *Crime Crab*!"

Sally, who plays the femme fatale in *Crime Crab,* ambled sideways down the aisle to accept her award for Best Supporting Actress in a Benthic Marine Crime Drama. In her breathy and exotic littoral accent, she said. "I vould like to sank all of zee cast and zee crew, and especially zee Barnacles who were always zere for me."

A clip from the season finale of *Crime Crab* comes up on the theater's screen. Sally's character, Dungeon-S, is hiding beside a sea anemone that perfectly matches her outfit. She blends in so well that even Crime Crab himself seems not to detect her as he approaches. The dramatic music fades and her internal voice says in a perfect mid-continental-shelf accent, "Come closer Crime Crab. That's it, keep coming. Who would think that one so skilled at playing both sides of the law would walk into a trap so easily?" She jumps out, spear-gun drawn. "So, Crime Crab – you thought you were getting a little action tonight, eh? Well, I have your action right here!"

"Baby, you should know better than to play games with me," says Crime Crab. And suddenly Chamois Shrimp swims toward Dungeon-S from the fan of a purple and white dappled gorgonian coral where he had been hiding in plain sight. He points his pistol claw at Dungeon-S.

She says, "You aren't so smart, Crime Crab. Don't you know never to bring a Shrimp to an Octopus fight?" Just then the large rock behind Chamois Shrimp becomes Artemis Octopus changing into his feeding colors. The frame freezes and TO BE CONTINUED scrolls across the screen.

Sally was genuinely moved and had to dab tears from her stalked eyes with her claw. She held up her trophy – a golden likeness of a plasmanoid imitating a humanoid. And she made sure to flash some major leg action for the cameras down front as she sashayed back to her seat.

Once the cheers died down the Master of Ceremonies, Grewv-The-Green-8, a pretty boy avianoid from Millet Fields-8, and host of the popular game show *The Newlyfledged Game*, said, "The fabulous, fabulous Sally Lightfoot! The hardest working actress in the intertidal! Okay folks, our next category is for best documentary featuring ignorance, intolerance, baseless vanity, and/or unsavory behavior. And the nominees are: *Backwoods Bigots*!"

A spotlight shined on the two three-legged bearded Rumbly-11 humanoid stars of *Backwoods Bigots*. They are tripodding in the foyer, apparently unable to tolerate sitting in a mixed-species audience.

"The second nominee is *Squirrel Squad*!"

A spotlight shined on a squad of young Squirrels down in the front rows. The males had painted their gray furry chests with orange block letters and arranged themselves to spell out *SQUARREL SQUID*. They pumped their fists and chattered. A buxom female Squirrel stood on her chair, pumped her fist, got tangled in her own tail, and fell into the seats behind her.

"Nicely done, as always, Squad," said the MC. "And the third nominee is *Translate This!* starring Dee-Ay-En-15 and produced by Trukk-9."

The spotlight shined down on Trukk-9 and Dee and their combined entourages. The lights lingered on the beautiful and radiant Fleence and Kyleence and their babies and toddlers. Michael and Gregory were asleep and looking very cute in their little churdleboy outfits. Miles peaked out of Kyleence's purse, chewing on something. Jimmy sported a lamé CC-logoed sport jacket, which tied-in nicely with the award show trophy.

"And the envelope please… The winner is… *Translate This!*"

Dee and Trukk-9 rose to huge applause. Caught up in the excitement, Dee gave Trukk-9 a friendly Bearman nudge. Trukk-9 left his feet and landed face-first on a music stand in the orchestra pit. Dee reached in and plucked Trukk-9 out. Blood streamed down Trukk-9's face. Dee placed him in front of the podium. The audience's applause died down and they began to murmur. Trukk-9 said, "It is but an insignificant laceration."

The theater screen played a clip from *Translate This!*

Trukk-9, in voice-over, says, "My great friend Dee appears about to fulfill his destiny!" Dee emerges from the packing peanuts. "He explodes like a wild lava rocket from a volcanic cloud. We can feel him erupting and launching free from the mountainous expanse of the clouded understanding caused by his nemesis, the vile and deceitful galactic autotranslator." The scene is now of Dee executing his perfect handstand at the top of the tower. "But poor Dee had merely soiled some other sort of device on top of a tower. It seems that his quest is only beginning..."

The scene switches to a montage of climactic moments from episodes of *Translate This!* Dee squats over some sort of vault. He is covered in honey, bits of forest duff, and a swarm of flies. Then he is swinging from a rope over a shed on an atoll with small dead fish and diving frigate birds shooting past his head. Then he is hanging from a cliff trying to get a shot at something in a cave when a powerful waterfall appears out of nowhere. Then Dee is swimming through choppy seas with powdered custard dropping from a chute in front of him. The water thickens around him. The song of a Dnooblian tenor climaxes, and Trukk-9's voice narrates again. "The galactic autotranslator's location remains a mystery. Heroic efforts, all for naught. Or were they…?" The screen goes dark.

The crowd cheered, Dee bowed, Trukk-9 refused medical care, the audience chanted for a speech. Dee stepped to the podium. "We'd like to thank our research assistant, former President Zelda-15." The spotlight found Zelda and Buster. They waved at the cameras, both dressed in Dab Tabmow cosplay.

"While Trukk-9 is still conscious, I think we should…" Dee looked at Grewv.

Grewv said, "Let's do this, baby!"

"Okay! Now what my buddy and esteemed colleague doesn't know is that we have a little surprise for him!"

"Oh, you shouldn't…" said Trukk-9.

"Yes my friend, the Institution and I are honored to present you with this lifetime achievement award!"

A high-grade Conversation Hostess with all the enhancements walked onstage with the trophy. It was a little golden replica of the Cruiser Duke Sukk-9 on a wooden stand. She bent down to place the trophy in Trukk-9's lap.

Dee said, "On behalf of the Institution, I present you with the inaugural Trukk-9 Lifetime of Achievement Lifetime Achievement Award!"

The lights dimmed and the audience quieted down as a retrospective video of the works of Trukk-9 came up on the big screen.

The music is a familiar acoustic guitar and tantric chant piece with Click Beetle percussion. Trukk-9 is seen being trampled by bulls on a narrow dusty street – Dee comes in at the end, camera on shoulder, to rescue his friend in case any more herds of bulls should appear. Trukk-9 is seen strapped to the outside of a small scout saucer with Dee visible through the viewing dome in the pilot's seat. They hit a swarm of locusts. Trukk-9 is buried up to his neck in sand. Dee loops a rope around Trukk-9's head and pulls him out using a harnessed churdle. Trukk-9 is somehow knocked from the side of Dee as they lean out to get footage of a raging river. He is dashed upon the rocks and swept downstream over a quarter-mile before they can reach him with a grabber beam. Now he is sprawled on the desert floor stuffing a scorpion into his mouth through cracked lips. Dee is seen in the background drinking bottled water and eating an energy bar. The next image is of Trukk-9 pulling leaches out from inside his rain slicker. Now he's in a cage fighting a Dnooblian algae bear. Then he's in the back of Jimmy's boat with a Mega-Mouth Poppin' Minnow hanging from three of his eyelids. And finally he's in his full Dab Tabmow costume being dragged by his head behind a crazed souvenir-hunting fanboy who thought his head was a prop.

The audience stood as one, cheering. Trukk-9 lifted his thumb.

Grewv the MC reclaimed the podium and announced, "And now, ladies and gentlemen, in celebration of Trukk-9's career, I give you *Snake Ape Night Boogie*!"

The house lights dimmed again and the ushers wheeled in a fluorescent force-field cage containing the star of *Snake Ape Night Boogie*, Victolicious Viper-14. The show's theme song came on with its instantly recognizable disco beat, and Vic-Vip broke into the sinuous and sensuous moves that got him where he is today. His fur emitted a beautiful bioluminescent blue-green color that shimmered as he boogied.

"It never fails to amaze me how one man with no limbs can boogie-down so," said the MC, as he himself began to boogie.

The ceremony deteriorated into an all-night disco party that people from across the Galactic Pool would be talking about for years. And many recipients had to receive their awards via mail, but they didn't mind. Some of these other winners included:

Mudhosh-X in the category of Best Feature Length Anime for his epic *Dragonmaster Kitten Versus the Undersea Vampire Zombie Unicorns.*

Slee-12 in the category of Best New Explosive-Themed Fishing Show for *Slee's Eelin' Hole, Uncut.*

Peggy, The Presidential Travelling Secretary for her after-school special *Granny's Greenhouse.*

Ambassador Dayv-19 and 'Blood' in the category of Documentary, Communing with Energy for their travel series *A Galaxy of Unsurfed Breaks, Daddy-O.*

Mutant Boy in the category of Best Supporting Actor for his role as Mutant Boy in *Dab Tabmow, ManCricket.*

Jacques 'Jimmy' Fresneaux in the category of Best Planetary Remodeling Series for *The Bass Ponds of New ZZZZZZ-3.*

Muffin Hen-19 and **Pip-The-Blue-8** for their series *Muffin Flock* in the category of Best Cooking Show, Real Food.

Michael-18 and Gregory-18 in the category of Best Original Series Concept for *Filligan's Island.*

O'Hecknid-3 and O'Jecknid-3 for their mini-series, *The Classic Literature of Planet One, Reinterpreted with Accidental Performances.*

'Dunger' and his old lady in the category of Best Transportation Series for *Extreme Pasture Rides.*

And **Captain O'Spotnid-3** with a posthumously-awarded Plasmy in the category of Best Adaptation for the screenplay of *I, Buzzy*. (Under contract to be produced by Trukk-9, and featuring Buster-15 as the young Buzzy.)

On the planet Earth we observed an activity called Cricket. I was not comfortable watching this so-called sport.
~ O'Buzznid-3

BOSTON'S FEET

The Big Voice Entity prowled a neighborhood in some random town in North America. He was looking for a house with the TV tuned to the news program that always talked about space aliens – the one with the blonde news anchor with the big feet. He didn't have to search for long.

His quantum thingularity consciousness occupied the living room of a man relaxing on a couch drinking a beer and still wearing his work clothes and boots. A deer head mounted on the wall seemed to watch ULBTX-123 wherever his consciousness tried to hover. He finally had to hover on top of the deer's head between the antlers to avoid its gaze.

"Welcome to Daily Today, Evening Edition. I'm Marie. Quickly I'd like to update you on our latest on-line viewer poll because it has a bearing on the composition of our show tonight. Due to certain confusions during the previous shows with our space alien expert panel, we asked you to help us make a cull by telling us which guests you believe most. Here are the results."

Marie saunters over to the big screen. An image of an aura-encircled hand emerging from a cloud appears on the screen with a big 15 next to it. "Fifteen percent agree with the Reverend Grace Goonch that the melting of Mount Rushmore was due to the Hand of the Almighty. Sorry, Grace, that's not enough to get on the panel today."

Then an aerial view of the Pentagon is displayed on the screen with a big 25 covering the center courtyard. Marie tosses her hair and says, "And twenty-five percent agree with Bob Gnobbler that shadowy puppet masters are announcing their final domination by targeting a code-forming series of symbolic targets – and that we need to decipher the code in order to stop them. Sorry Bob, apparently seventy-five percent of our viewers are willing to endure eternal subjugation by our own home-grown dark forces."

Then an image of a flying saucer about to be caught in Merle 'Doc' Maudlin's stranglehold grip comes up on the screen with the number 30 superimposed on his bicep like a tattoo.

"And thirty percent agree with the host of *Grab That Thing Before It Gets Away*, 'Doc' Maudlin. You say that it must be space aliens." The studio audience cheers, and Marie has to ask them to stop chanting.

Then a big question mark comes up on the screen with the number 30 in its crook. "And thirty percent either believe it was something else, think the question was still last week's poll when we asked for your favorite pizza topping, or they simply couldn't make up their minds in the face of overwhelming evidence. We gave all those votes to Doctor Oscar Boston. So please welcome our guests – 'Doc' Maudlin and Doctor Oscar!"

'Doc' Maudlin bounds onto the set pumping his arms in his trademark thing-grabbing motion. Doctor Boston somehow ends up in his own chair without anyone noticing how he got there.

ULBTX-123 was distraught. Thirty percent! If the Chancellery finds out… I'm sunk, he thought. He continued to watch, desperate to come up with some way to hide or bury this.

"What's the latest evidence for space aliens 'Doc'?" asks Marie.

"I'm glad you ask, Marie. You may have heard about the gigantic blue feather that a fisherman found on some lake somewhere not too long ago."

A picture comes up on the screen of a guy standing on a dock all decked out in branded bassin' apparel. He holds a meter-long blue feather out in front of himself so the perspective makes the feather look even bigger.

"Tests on this feather show that it is an alien species. Proof, Marie. We now know that they are feathered aliens. Either that or they have large pet birds. OR, and this is somewhat controversial, they could be shape-shifters. Experts are watching the feather closely, just in case." The crowd murmurs.

"So what do you have to say about that, Doctor Boston?" asks Marie.

"This is a very interesting feather, Marie. Genetic tests show that it is an unknown species, but it shares ninety-eight percent of its DNA with the common budgerigar, or budgie, or also called common parakeet."

"Make up your mind, Boston. You can't have everything," says 'Doc'. "Birds of a feather flock together!" The audience cheers as if 'Doc' has just landed a knock-out punch.

"What I'm saying is, Marie, is that this odd feather comes from something that originated on THIS planet. It could be an extreme mutant, some sort of hybrid, or possibly a genetic experiment that escaped. It is very unlikely to be from a militant race of giant space budgies."

Marie says, "We've got a live update from our on-line viewer poll. All of the Goonch and Gnobbler votes have switched in favor of 'Doc' Maudlin and the space aliens. The vote on the cause of the melting of Mount Rushmore now stands as eighty-percent space aliens, fifteen-percent don't know, and five percent pepperoni!"

'Doc' does his pose, and Doctor Boston plants his palm on his forehead, which has inadvertently become his trademark pose.

"If that's not scientific, then I don't know what is," says Marie. "You can't argue with the numbers. I suppose the next question is when are they going to contact us, and how friendly are they going to be."

Noooooooooooooooooooo thought ULBTX-123. I have to preempt this. I need to find this Doctor Boston…

ULBTX-123 followed the signal through the wires and airwaves and entered the studio where Doctor Boston was just about to leave the building. He followed the Doctor right out the back door, to his modest automobile, and tracked him into the night all the way home.

***

"Psst – hello," said ULBTX-123 in his littlest voice.

Doctor Boston startled awake. "WHA!?" He clapped twice and the light came on. "Who is that? Where are you?"

"Ah, you are indeed a good scientist – asking lots of questions. That's good – very good indeed."

"Is this some kind of gag? Who are you? Where are you?"

"No, Doctor Boston, I assure you, this is no gag. But before I answer your questions, tell me – how big are your feet?"

"What? Come on – I'm calling the cops."

"Okay, you want proof that this isn't a hoax of some kind? Look out the window and peer into the night sky. I'll be right back."

Doctor Boston watched as a huge fireball trailing beautiful blue sparks traversed the sky.

"Whoa!!"

"Pretty neat trick, eh?"

"Alright then, who are you?"

"Foot size, Doctor. Foot size, please…"

"Uh, size ten, why?"

"Have you ever worn a size ten-and-a-half?"

"I have a pair of slippers in size ten-and-a-half."

"Do they fit?"

"Well enough, yes, they are comfortable."

"So if we were to round the decimal up, that would make you a size eleven, right?"

"If you insist. Now tell me who you are."

"Very good – size eleven will do nicely. My name is Space Pirate-X, but I go by many other names. My official designation is Upper Left Buttocks-123, but my friends call me 123. Some also call me Big Voice Entity, Mister Loudy, The Headless Hung-Like-A-Horse Man, and even Alrighty Almighty on one planet."

His avatar appears in the bedroom, hovering and rotating in front of Doctor Boston.

"If it really was aliens, I guess I'll have to eat some crow on TV now."

"Not necessarily, Doctor Boston, not necessarily… The aliens are finished with Earth. I took care of them. Now we need each other's help to convince everyone that it was something else. You got any ideas?"

"Why would I want to do that? Actual space aliens visiting Earth is the biggest news in history. It doesn't matter what I WANT to believe. I believe what the evidence tells me is most likely correct. And right now I'm seeing pretty convincing evidence of aliens. But show me one more thing to seal it, please."

"Okay, I'll be right back. There, now look out on your lawn. See the meteorite?"

Doctor Boston walked out front. Sure enough, there was a fog-shrouded rock about as big as a laundry basket on the lawn next to his bird feeder. It was coated in ice even though it was a balmy evening. He came back inside, flabbergasted.

"So what exactly is it that you want from me?"

"I understand that it might be frustrating to have made the biggest discovery in history and not be able to prove it. But I can make that up to you several-fold, Doctor. I'll tell you the missing secrets of matter and energy. I'll provide you with mathematical proofs – the nature of dark matter and so-on. You will win all the big science awards, and your new status will allow you to convince everyone that space aliens are not responsible for anything. We'll figure out what you should say later."

"I'm a scientist dedicated to finding the truth, Mister Buttocks. Tell me your secrets, and then I'll decide."

"You have to promise not to use this information to try and produce a new Big Bang, alright? All I need you to do is publish the paper that will demonstrate its theoretical possibility."

"So then what's to stop someone else from using the information to cause another Big Bang?" asked Doctor Boston.

"ME!"

"Shhhhh! Damn, you'll wake the neighbors."

"I will be watching. I'm ALWAYS watching. But if anyone asks where you came up with these ideas, you DO NOT mention me," said ULBTX-123.

"No one would believe it anyway."

"I don't mean Earthlings, Doctor Boston. Now listen carefully..."

My life will soon come to an end. But do not cry, for I probably did not like you anyway.
~ O'Buzznid-3

ON THE RUN

If you saw him, you wouldn't suspect that this man was the Galactic Pool's most wanted fugitive. You'd never guess that this man had committed deeds so heinous that no one had ever thought to come up with laws against them. It would never occur to you that this man could be responsible for a planet-wide plague of hooves. This man was so beaten that you might not even guess his species – perhaps a Fermamentian or a Scablander even…? And you'd laugh if someone said he had once been one of the richest and most powerful men in the Galactic Pool. In looking at him, all you'd probably notice was an angry and broken old man.

But Griffer-1 was still Griffer-1. And there were still a few high-placed people around that he could extort by way of certain bits of delicate information. This is how Griffer-1 found himself standing in the PLUMBOB motor pool hangar all by himself.

All of the flying saucers were the same kind. Some were a little more worn than others, and a few were in various stages of repair. All were equipped with memory wipers, cloaking devices, medical duplicators, probaluators, and high capacity egocite and calming agent systems. All were capable of interstellar travel and were programmed with military-grade charts and navigation systems. The only reason to be picky about which one to steal was how much fuel was in the tank.

He just needed to go to a place where he could start over. He needed a place full of rubes to manipulate – where no one would recognize him – a place where he could turn the screws again. And a guy like him with a ship like this could probably take over a planet like that. Of course, he already knew this place.

Griffer-1 found a ship with the needle on full. He tapped the gage a couple of times to make sure. He booted the computer. He turned the main power switch on.

Then Griffer-1 looked up and noticed his crooked smile reflected in the saucer's viewing dome.

"Computer, take me to Dirt," he said.

"Do you mean 'Soil' or perhaps 'Earth'?" replied the computer.

"Fuck fuck fuck fuck fuck fuck! Earth. I think..."

GUIDE TO THE PLANETS OF THE GALACTIC POOL

Planet One – Somewhat cat-like small-footed and/or hooved humanoids
Bounty-2 – Displaced Earthling control group (location deduced/seduced)
ZZZZZZ-3 – The insectoid world with many intelligent species and a fresh makeover
Fermament-4 – Complexly symmetrical odoriferous nosey humanoids, still
Blue-5 – Ancient plasmanoids who seem kind of different no matter how well shape-shifted
Cache-6 – Carnivorous Squirrel People who eat a different kind of nut, and are nuts
Precipice-7 – Goat People who enjoy having hooves (thank-you very naying much)
Millet Fields-8 – Slender and elegant avianoids, galaxy's 2nd best boogiers, 98% budgie
Bukk-9 – Copiously-eyed and antlered humanoids, total population level unknown
Dnooblia-10 – Home of the Dnooblians, minus a couple
Rumbly-11 – Stout three-legged humanoids with massively thick values
Swampy-12 – Home of the Swamp Masters, relatively icky
Flat Rock-13 – Sequentially hermaphroditic Crab People (Crime Crab is now Christine Crab)
Peat-14 – Snake Apes, bioluminescent, boogieluminescent
Free-15 – Ursoid Bear People planet with rapidly increasing population of Crickets and kittens
Sphere-16 – Ichthyoid Mudskippers with fingers, still finding their place in the galaxy
Scablands-17 –Two hands on one arm and bony hook on other, but not denied health insurance

Chuffed-18 – Colony of cloned former slaves and egocite miners – now gamete miners
Mother Roost-19 – Large flightless avianoid former dinosaurs, stoked
Earth – Still a player…

CHAPTERS OF BOOK III (MAYBE)

An Eel by Any Other Name
My Mind to Your Mind – Your Thoughts to This Hard Drive
Dungtona 500
Michael's and Gregory's First Day of School
I, Buzzy at the Box Office
Galactic Largemouth Bass Invasion! Bassin' Men Needed!
Shouldn't Have Grabbed That Thing Before It Got Away
Big Bang Roulette
Stolen from Earth – You Too?
Bucking Bronto
Squirrel Squad on the Loose!
Overworked Cavemen
Ketchup-18 – Year's Most Popular Child's Name, Girl
Mutant Boy and Mutant Girl, an Awkward Romance
Mudskippers, Make Up Your Minds
Honk Around The Clock!
Sally Lightfoot Sex Tape
Dinosaurs in the Line-up
Bigfoot Comes Clean
Griffer-1 – Evil Dolphin (naw)
Duplicator Accidentally Left On
PSST - Need Seed?
Are You Sure You're Sapient?
New Beat: Doot Honk Doot Honk Doot Honk Doot Doot
Antlers Fashionable Again
Does Your Species Wear Pants?
Boogie by Decree
The Muffin Revolution
Now THAT'S A Budgie!
How Many Vice Presidents Are In There?
Blacksmiths Make Natural Grabber Beam Operators
Panspermia, After Hours

ABOUT THE AUTHOR

M. Sid Kelly grew up in a globe-crawling military family with his English mum and a Californian dad who engineered Air Force base TV stations. So young Sid grew up surrounded by TVs – with British comedies, U.S. fishing shows, and 1970's Tagalog-language kung fu movies competing for the best naughty bits. He graduated with a four-year degree in marine biology eight years after enrolling at Humboldt State University. Having completed two years in Africa with the Peace Corps, he got a job as federal fisheries bureaucrat - until too many dead fish had piled up. Now he consults on fish protection measures for bridge construction projects in order to pay the bills, and he wrote Used Aliens and Freed Aliens in order to become a zillionaire one day. His conclusion after having run around all over the place looking at stuff: Space aliens are going to think we are the weird ones.

***

OTHER BOOKS BY M. SID KELLY:

USED ALIENS – A NOVEL

In case you chose to start with book two (this one), Used Aliens is the first Galactic Pool book, and it can be found here:

U.S. http://www.amazon.com/dp/B00BJ602QQ
U.K. https://www.amazon.co.uk/dp/B00BJ602QQ
Lovely Canada: https://www.amazon.ca/dp/B00BJ602QQ
Awesome Australia: https://www.amazon.com.au/dp/B00BJ602QQ

***

TIGERFISH! Stories from Two Years Fishing in West Africa

Here's the blurb:

If you go to live on the Niger River in West Africa, don't forget your pole, your sense of humor, and your camera!

Provides answers to these important questions:

How do you handle a certain electric fish, and what if you screw up?

What happens when a cobra tries to get in the boat?

Which one lure will catch tigerfish, Nile perch, catfish, Tilapia, etc?

Where do you catch a tigerfish, and how do you deal with its teeth?

When is a fish going to kill you if you eat it?

Who might you meet, and what are they saying?

A two-year account of sport and traditional fishing by a fish biologist Peace Corps Volunteer in Mali, West Africa.

This photo-journal contains 19,000 words and 140 color photographs. It opens with sport fishing, and details the author's pursuit of tigerfish, Nile perch, and other species including the dubious dodo.

The second part is an account of experiences and observations made during the large community fishing events that take place in the waters of the floodplain during the dry season.

The third section provides a brief description and numerous pictures of the life and work of small-scale commercial Somono fishers.

The final section documents two traditional fire hunts on the Niger River floodplain.

The quality of photos is better than most pictures of the Loch Ness Monster...

TIGERFISH! Available as an ebook here:

http://www.amazon.com/dp/B00H7XPCI8

***

The disclaimer: Except for arguably Werner Herzog as Trukk-9, the characters are the product of the author's imagination. Any resemblance to other actual persons – Earthling or alien, living or dead – is purely coincidental. However, if you think you resemble Gren Wee-1, Griffer-1, Gro Skoo-1, or Rim Ram-1, then you should consider suing the author. Gregory and Michael – you owe us, so if you don't like the use of your names, images, personalities, ailments, insecurities, and direct quotes, tough.

*And apologies to Vera Matson and Lionel Newman for totally ripping off their 1964 Daniel Boone Theme Song, which the author sort-of remembers from his childhood…

16068029R00143

Made in the USA
Middletown, DE
03 December 2014